DAVI

of legal age
not diagnosed

Flávia Menegaz

Cover / Supervision
Dilce Laranjeira

Translation
Alana Irigaray and Alec Irigaray

First published in Brazil 2019 by Flávia Menegaz
Original title: Davi, maior de idade, não diagnosticado
ISBN 979-8591563226

Independently Published

Inscription

To all those who suffer the profound and unconditional
silence of their own minds, to the uncomprehended,
to the discriminated, ignored, and forgotten.
To my beloved Davi.

I'm learning to fly
inner and calm flights

In the garden of silences
spring up transparent responses

In tune with infinite beings
transparent meetings spring up

Two minutes of Nirvana with Davi
Wales, March of 2018

CONTENT

Foreword   9

Introduction   11

Chapter 1   13

Chapter 2   17

Chapter 3   29

Chapter 4   31

Chapter 5   47

Chapter 6   65

Chapter 7   73

Chapter 8   89

Chapter 9   97

Chapter 10   101

Chapter 11   125

Chapter 12   139

Chapter 13   147

Chapter 14   157

Chapter 15   163

Chapter 16   165

Acknowledgments   177

References   179

About the author   181

Foreword

Depression: We need to talk about it

When Flávia honored me with the manuscript of her book, I felt obliged to write something about it. First, I congratulated her, because I imagine how much it must hurt to touch her wounds for the greater good: to make her pain a learning experience so that other people don't have to feel the same. Secondly, I encouraged her, because we need to talk about the "disease of the century," the one that kills more than AIDS, stroke or acute myocardial infarction, and that, even so, when using her worst clothing, surrounded with "pre-concept" threads, remains a stain without a tumor or laboratory alteration.

It takes not only courage but also a domain to talk about depression. Not long ago, analyzing the work of Jean Clair, art historian and curator of the exhibition **Melancholy**, who studied the artistic approaches of depression, I concluded that we don't understand the melancholy as much as the Greeks. Our time denies it. You have to be happy, funny, fun, positive, and in that context, depression is forbidden. The ideal man stays constant all the time, without mood changes, such as fruits and vegetables in the supermarket, which always have the same color, the same size, and the same taste.

And that's why we've been trying to fight the "prejudice" for a long time because it kills! Every time someone finishes saying "depression is fussiness" or "depression doesn't exist," someone commits suicide in the world: one person per second, according to recent WHO data. In Brazil, every 45 minutes, a person is a victim of suicide, causing it to become a public health issue, and this rate has only increased in recent years, especially among young males between 15 and 30 years old.

This may be the last stage of pain that a human being can feel, and knowing that 90% of these cases can be avoided (still according to the WHO) is what causes massive campaigns such as "Yellow September" or "Psychophobia is Crime" to be created by the Brazilian Psychiatric Association.

That being said, information is the best kind of prevention.

I believe that Flávia has the noble goal of reaching as many people as possible because the world needs to know that depression has a name, treatment, and cure; that it can affect anyone so that everyone is vulnerable; that there are numerous causes, involving even chemical issues so that they feel encouraged to seek help.

This is what Davi would wish.

If you are a person who still doubts that depression is a disease that should be taken very seriously, continue reading. If, by the end, you're not convinced, all I ask is that you don't judge, discriminate or diminishes it.

If you knew how much it hurts, I'm sure you wouldn't do it.

Raphael Menezes
Psychiatric Medic – Specialized by the Paranaense Institution
of Behavioral Therapy

Introduction

When he said, **"You can tell everything, Mom. This book will help many people"**, the fear stunned me for exposing the fragility of a son, whose cheerful, restless, and insightful mind sadly fell ill, dissipated.

May parents, brothers, friends, teachers, social workers, doctors, police, lawyers, judges, politicians, religious individuals, all people, take advantage of this history, this life, to understand better and act.

We need to change our perception, our attitudes, our books. We need to discuss mental health in classrooms, decimate prejudices, show appropriate prevention, support, and treatment possibilities. Get to know the human mind better, chemical imbalances, brain connections/disconnections that can negatively modify our thinking, our behavior, by being essential so that we can commit ourselves, when needed, to "seek back" the person we indeed are, or someone who is suffering alongside us.

We need to change the laws, public policies, so that diseases of the mind, whether they are simple or complex, which affect millions of human beings, must not be ignored. Let the rescue arrive on time. Let there be a proper scientific investment so that these lives are possible.

These would undoubtedly be some effective measurements in suicide prevention.

Thank you, my beloved son, Davi, for your valuable generosity, allowing me to share such difficult moments for the benefit of your fellow equals.

Chapter 1

In the midst of one of the difficult phases of my life, I wrote poems. Poems for teenagers, airy poems, humorous, with doses of hope. But on the outside, a maxim echoed, bittering my days: "We are responsible for our choices." Put it this way, loosen, it sounded like an alert lighting up my senses; after all, it is much responsibility imposed with brutal simplicity. Having said my failures countless times, was its consolidation, which, above all, forced those around me to pay for my mistakes since I could not bear all the responsibility for my wrong choices.

I look out the window, see the slum. A girl knocks door to door, asking for change. Holding a baby in her arms, one still in her womb, others in the dumpster, or wandering the streets. By living in a troubled environment having no emotional structure, she can't see any future. Having urgent needs, affections, and pressing disaffections. I believe she was chosen to express certain injustices of the world.

Running away is feasible. Escape this trap, change the direction...I have an enormous inner strength, born and raised in the impossible days. Maybe here, right now, what distances me from this girl is called "luck."

I am alone, depressed, and unemployed in the borrowed apartment where I live with my ten and twelve-year-old. My twenty-year-old daughter lives with my parents on the next block. My attempts to get out of chaos have not taken me anywhere and writing poems at the bottom of the well is completely insane, but it was what relieved me.

I counted the coins on the table. I did not want to borrow money again. Everyone knew I had not been able to pay for years. The phone and the power was about to be cut again. I called the publisher, hoping that there would be some money to receive: "You know, poetry books are challenging to sell ..." I called the lawyer for news about the alimony process: "There is nothing to do, Flávia, we have to wait for the deadlines set by Justice."

I remembered the woman crouched, with a baby sucking on her breast, in line at the Public Defender's Office screaming: "How many years will I have to wait? When my son grows up, I will have done it myself! What the fuck is this Justice?" Taking care of everything alone may not be a heroic act as it seems. It can cost a lot of time away from the child trying to seek support; it can cost physical and emotional overload, frustration, anger, revolt, resentment, impatience, parental alienation, alcoholism, and other imbalances. And the baby was there, sucking on injustices... One by one. One morning, when the boys were at school, I stood staring at the table and the many years of working as a teacher, the storytelling that I was desperately trying to sell, the resumés, the diplomas, the book... I took it all, crumpled it, and threw it on the floor, leaving the table clean. Then I took an empty sheet of paper and started writing painful poems — *Reversos*, a book I never published.

> *I have a well-cared plantation of failures*
> *on the droughts or floods*
> *they grow.*
> *On my fierce tongue,*
> *flowers moan*
> *and fruits ignite during the harvest*

"Children overcome everything". I relieved my pain in the words of a friend who tried to help me during the interminable crises of my marriage. When I saw them playing and smiling, I thought everything was fine. Suffering is part of a human being's life. Some, however, can be avoided, minimized, transformed into affections, and they must be, after all, there are certain wounds that, together with other wounds, make the soul sick and can kill.

𝄢:

On an unexpected Monday, I received a call from the publisher. My book had been chosen by The National School Library Program. The government was buying about twenty thousand copies. Among hundreds of books, having the work recognized is the dream of any author. Even so, I could not dance around the apartment as if I had a thin dress in a sunny field.

A few weeks later, the ten percent I had from copyrights was in my bank account. That meant precisely thirteen thousand reais. That money did not solve my problem. Of course, it was very welcomed; however, it was not enough to change my life, and I needed to change it at all costs. I went to an old neighbor's house to ask for advice and information. She had already lived in Europe. No, I won't stay here anymore. My country has already whipped enough. I will take the prize it has been given me and run away before it steals it from me and throws me in the mud again. The prospect of a just life excited me. I imagined my children studying, graduating abroad, happy, fulfilled, with dozens of opportunities ahead of them. And I, without ever suffering for being a burden on people's lives, being able to be the owner of me, the structure that the children needed to grow without the deprivations that limited them, without the anguish of an uncertain future. For that reality, I would fight with all my strength.

From the bus window that took me to the plane, the live photograph of the farewell: my parents and my three children were waving at me. I walked down the corridor as it pulled away, looking for one last look, feeling the pain of a photograph tearing and wetting my face, my body and, my heart.

Chapter 2

During the night, I crossed the Atlantic and other borders. In my eyes, they broke, one by one, reflecting the map on the small screen in the armchair in front of me. I stepped, I stepped with my body and soul on that foreign soil, at the so desired opportunity. The humid air, the people of different nationalities at the airport, the signs, the products on the shelves, the hot water on the tap in the bathroom... I felt myself entering another reality, new, different, exciting, and immense happiness took over me.

I was in England! The opposite direction of the driver, of traffic: going instead of coming! A feeling that things were in the wrong place, but they were right and could be even better. There were other ways of living that I had yet known, and it fascinated me. At the entrance to the city of Brighton, under the streetlights, I saw the first typical English houses — beautiful, cozy. Me, a living, real character from my film. Everything filled me with admiration, and there would be many surprises on my way.

I arrived at Lisa's house at dawn. Her husband, a little sleepy, disheveled, came to see me. In a carpeted hallway, several pairs of shoes were lined up on the floor — I thought it was strange. He showed me the room, where I just leaned on the suitcase and threw myself on the bed, exhausted and delirious. The next morning, I found Lisa in the living room. Beautiful, young, caring. She showed me the house, explained how to turn on the oven, the space in the fridge where I could keep my food, gave me the key, and left for work, in a skirt and sandals, while I shivered in my wool blouse.

I went out to look for a payphone. The houses, with large glass windows, gardens, low walls, without bars, without electric fences — what a surprise! The payphone on the corner ate my coins, but I could speak to my mom for a few seconds, just enough to say that I had arrived well and know if my children Joyce, Israel, Davi and her were fine.

When Lisa and her husband came home from work, they took me for a drive around town. Everything was stunning to me. I had a feeling that I had been stuck all those past years and that I was now free. I realized how isolated Brazil is from the rest of the planet. Their size and geographic location make it practically impossible for Brazilian people to live extraordinary cultural experiences like the one I was living unless one could pay dearly for them.

— There are no poor people here! — I said to the couple, who laughed at my naivety.

— Yes, there are many! — they replied. I understood that our concepts about the poor and poverty were quite different.

The friendly couple were friends with my former neighbor. They rented rooms for students and gave me some contacts from foreigners with whom I could relate, ask for suggestions. Through these contacts, I met a Brazilian woman who had been there for a few months and she gave me several tips. I left bills paid in Brazil and a certain amount for expenses during my absence. Apart from the costs of my ticket and the rent for that room, I had almost nothing left, just twenty pounds for food. I would have little time to get a job; otherwise, I would have no other option but my return ticket within a month. I made my resumé and walked around, handing it out door to door. The service would be simple, and I was prepared for it: cleaning houses, hotel rooms, or helping in the kitchen of some restaurant — I did not care. It was the month of May, the temperature rising, summer arriving, the most anticipated, and busiest time of the year.

Brighton is an artistic, touristic, university, eclectic city, full of English courses that welcomed students from different countries around the world. The streets overflowed with diversity. There is ample freedom of expression in the English culture, exotic hair, clothes, tattoos, and piercings among young and old. Only the visual is enough to cause what they call "culture shock". Amazed and worried, I thought: "Will my children adapt here?"

Lisa's house was around a forty-minute walk from the center, which was not bad for those who still had great distances to wander. I was surviving on the biscuit and milk I bought at Poundland, a store where everything costs a pound. My second week in the city already meant half the time I had to get a job, and certain desperation started to surround me. In addition to delivering resumés, I also started looking for a job in the newspapers, but I had a hard time talking on the phone. Asking questions was not difficult; it was complicated to understand the answers, with spoken English, the expressions, the accents. The possibility of coming back with another failure to carry was turning into despair. At the end of the afternoon, I left for another onslaught. I used to walk through lanes, real mazes of alleys in the city center, an ancient and very charming part, which had already been a small fishing village for many years and nowadays is full of shops, cafes, pubs, and restaurants.

I looked at the frontage of a restaurant, with a resumé in hand when a boy approached me:

— *Ciao, bella! Pizza* or *pasta* for just six pounds!

— I would love to — I replied feeling a little embarrassed — but I have no money, I'm looking for a job.

— Ah, come, come with me — he said, leading me by the shoulder to a nearby table on the sidewalk, where a big man with gray hair and a serious face was.

— *Papà*, she is looking for a job.

— Do you have a resumé?

I handed it over, saying:

— I already worked at a family restaurant in Brazil.

He looked for a moment.

— Can you start tomorrow?

— Yes, I can!

Jumps of joy! I did not have a cell phone back then. It was still a luxury for me. I went to the nearest Internet cafe, to give the news to my loved ones in Brazil: I got a job!

A great surprise was to find two Brazilians in the restaurant's kitchen, Jorge and Luciana. They helped me a lot, taught me how to prepare food and the meaning of words I didn't know. The boss was a stupid, impolite Italian who could only swear and scream. He didn't have the slightest patience when things weren't exactly as he imagined.

In the rush hours, that small, stuffy kitchen underground became true hell. I tried my best to keep him from getting too stressed out with me, but I was new, my experience with restaurants was at the counter and serving at the tables. I found out there that I had slow movements and short arms for that kind of service. I had to be very quick and keep in mind the orders that came one after the other — salads, sandwiches, and starters — between the shouting of the chefs and the waiters...I didn't think I could handle it. My legs hurt after ten, twelve hours standing, and I was still walking forty minutes to Lisa's house. Lying in bed, exhausted, could not close my hands, swollen from carrying so many heavy dishes. "I'm not giving up... I have to get used to it."

The greatest football championship on Earth had begun, and people were agitated. I was cast to work the night shift that week. When I got to the kitchen, there was no one, just a big mess. Soon after, the boss arrived, the rude Italian. When he saw it, he started shouting throwing on the ground everything that was in front of him. Without saying anything, I bent down and started picking up the canisters and the vegetables. When I was getting up, a sack of potatoes almost hit my face. I stopped for a moment, astonished. I went up the stairs ripping off my apron. Saw the manager and said, "I need 15 minutes." I left without giving further explanation. I went to the beach that was only a block away and cried. I cried, longing for my children. "Humiliation... I just want a dignified life...What am I supposed to do? I have nowhere to go, and I have no money nor choice…". I stayed there until I calmed down. I took a deep breath..." I'll go back to the restaurant and do my job in the best possible way."

It had been half an hour, and I did not even realize it. As I was walking down the stairs towards the kitchen, I encountered the restaurant owner, who, when he saw me, yelled at me to leave and not come back. I did not try to explain. I thought it was better that way. I looked right at him and said, *"Thank you very much"*, as if he was doing me a favor, and left.

There were only two days left before I had to leave Lisa's house.

The room had already been rented to a student. I had nowhere else to stay nor money. I went back to the restaurant the next day to charge for the days worked. Their facial expressions were not good for me. Jorge came to give me a sermon because I "abandoned" the kitchen to watch the Brazilian match. That was the conversation that circulated there. I explained what had happened. "I just want my money to pay for some accommodation, and I'm going to look for another job."

The place where Luciana was living was crowded. Jorge asked me to wait for him. He took me to his flat, downtown, to meet his wife and his eight-year-old daughter. At the entrance, we walked through a narrow corridor stepping on the garbage left by the pub staff that operated on the first floor, scattered by the seagulls, who were always hungry and tore the bags which were left out of the large dumpster, causing a bad first impression. It was a small flat, in which the couple and their daughter shared the same room.

— You won't stay on the streets! — said his wife Joana, with a determined voice and generous look. — We will put a mattress here for you in this corner until things work out.

— Thank you, dear...— I thanked her with a hug.

She worked at a large beachfront restaurant and referred me to her boss, who was hiring more staff for the summer season. Filled with joy, which made her even more vibrant, Joana entered the flat screaming:

— Flávia! Flávia! I got you a job at the restaurant! You start the day after tomorrow!

— Really?! Oh, that's wonderful! — we celebrated with leaps of joy — But at the restaurant, they ask for a European document.

I sat on the bed discouraged.

— I don't have any... My Italian citizenship hasn't come out yet...

— Don't worry, and it can be worked out.

At night, when Jorge arrived, he phoned some contacts. Then he pulled out an old cell phone and handed me along with a piece of paper and a few pounds.

— You can pay me back later. Go to London tomorrow and get the document you need.

21

— Isn't it dangerous?

— Don't worry, and it's just to present it at the restaurant. It's a good place to work. If you don't have a document, people will make a slave out of you around here. A lot of workers won't even get paid and don't have a way to appeal for justice. Do you want to work or go back to the shitty situation you were in Brazil? We get rough here, and we kick ass in these restaurants... We just want a chance, don't we? So work, work to change your life and your children's.

I took the train to London as planned. I was trying to follow the signs, the names of the cities. I couldn't understand the audio ads. I got to Victoria Station and called the boy. He gave me the name of another station. So, I did, four times until he asked me to meet him at a diner.

— Stay around. As soon as it's ready, I'll phone you.

I walked around the neighborhood streets. Tired, I saw a park with a large lawn. I then sat there, waiting for the phone call. A man who seemed Bolivian approached me and started a conversation:

— You're Latina, aren't you?

— I'm Brazilian.

— Have you come here for four tourism?

— I'm living in Brighton. I've come to meet a friend. I forgot a document I need to present it at my new job tomorrow. And you, do you live here?

— Yes, I've been living here for a year now. I work in a cleaning company. My life in Bolivia was very difficult. I'm far away from my wife and son, but I can at least send them some money.

— Yes... Life isn't easy, I know...

After telling him about my first days in London, he asked me to write down his name and phone number.

— If there is ever anything, I can help you with, call me, at least I'm here longer than you are!

— Ivo... Thank you, Ivo!

I walked around the park, the streets but no news from the man. I looked at my watch, and it was almost 7 p.m. So, I decided to call:

— So, is it going to take too long?

— I'll give it to you tomorrow.

— Tomorrow? I've been here waiting for hours! You said you would call me, and you didn't!

— There is nothing that can be done today.

— But I live in Brighton!

— I'm sorry, but tomorrow at 8 a.m. at the same cafe.

I called Jorge.

— What should I do, Jorge? Get a train back to Brighton or wait until tomorrow?

— The problem Flávia, is that the train tomorrow before 10 a.m. is too expensive, and you have to be here to start at the restaurant, but what can be done?

— Ok, I have an idea, we will talk later.

I called Ivo.

— My friend had a problem, and couldn't meet me today, and I've only got 20 pounds, it's not enough to go back to Brighton and come back tomorrow.

He realized my anxiousness, and on the attempt to understand each other, he was speaking Castilian and I Portuguese.

— Wait for me in front of the park. I will meet you there.

Fifteen minutes later, there he was.

— Do you want some money to rent a hotel room?

— No, that would be too expensive, I don't want to borrow money, I would just like a place for me to spend the night, a couch.

— The owner of the house I'm living at is a Brazilian woman. Let's talk to her.

He had a seemed very peaceful and had good manner. Spoke slow-ly, had a look of someone who knew what I was suffering. It was enough for me to trust him. The Brazilian wasn't there. He tried to call, but there was no answer. We went to the kitchen, where he prepared a ham sandwich and a glass of refreshment. The house was very simple, and there was no living room. All three rooms were rented.

— You can sleep on my bed; I'll set up on the floor.

He had almost nothing, only a backpack and a blanket.

— No, that's not fair…

The other two people who were in the house at the time also had no mattress nor blanket. I made my jacket as a pillow, covered myself with a wool blouse that he lent me, and laid there on the carpet. Then I texted Jorge with the address I was at.

At eight o'clock, I picked up my document and ran to the station. I called Joana to tell her I was going to be late for my first day on the job.

— Don't worry; I've explained everything to the boss. It's alright.

— What a relief! I can't miss the opportunity!

I walked in, a little clumsy after so much running, in the huge kitchen of the restaurant, everyone was looking at me; they welcomed me, I handed the document to the manager, put on the uniform and started working.

The night at the flat was exciting: Joana, Jorge, the little girl, an Italian, Márcio, a Brazilian who also lived there, and me, gathered in a lively conversation in the lobby, where I told them my little adventure and celebrated my new job with my new friends.

Two months before my trip to England, I hired a young lady, who I already knew, to take care of the apartment and the boys in Brazil. Even with Joyce deploying among brothers, university, friends, and the constant supervision of my mom, over time, things began to go off the rails...My parents then decided to close the apartment and take the boys to live with them.

My departure entailed several changes. I needed to keep my mind focused on my goal and make sure that in the end, every sacrifice would be worth it. I had a new job, just ten minutes away from Jorge and Joana's house. I would go to the beach on sunny mornings, breathing with happiness all that wonderful opportunity that was happening in my life. When Márcio, the Brazilian, left, I shared the attic he rented with the nephew of the couple a cheerful and fun boy. It was a good way to save money. After paying my debt to Jorge, I raised some money for the first time and bought gifts for Joyce and my parents and Nike cleats for the boys. In Brazil, that was out of my reach. I always bought cheap, counterfeit, lousy sneakers with peddlers. The feeling of conquest, acquiring something with my effort, made me experience what I understood by dignity. I didn't mind doing simple jobs, cutting vegetables, washing dishes, cleaning toilets, as long as they gave me what my diploma and years of work had never given me. I wonder how many people around the world spend their lives with no chance of change as a result of an unfair system.

First World... How much respect for human beings! Arriving at the health center and touching the computer screen to confirm the consultation, the name of the doctor who would see me and how many minutes — not many — I would have to wait, seated, in a decent, large, carpeted room is like going to a private office in Brazil. Everything amazed me: the politeness of the English, always saying "thank you" or "sorry" for any small gesture made, being able to walk down the street without the fear of being robbed, sitting on the grass of the squares and parks to relax, walking on the second floor of the red buses, discovering beautiful places on the outskirts and have a pint of beer at the pubs to celebrate! On the other hand, the longing for Brazilian food, our rice and beans, the music... How I missed the music! The Internet was still restricted. I asked Joyce to mail me some CDs. Listen to Brazilian music in a foreign land is different; it made me feel who I truly was.

There was a large assemble of waiters and waitresses at the restaurant. Most were only there for a few months; they were students or just wanted to gain some experience for their resumé. They were young people from Poland, Spain, Italy, Portugal, Canada, Australia, Brazil. A Brazilian waiter encouraged me to take my children to school in Brighton.

— That's all I wanted, but I'm not sure. The culture is very different, and I think it would be a very big shock.

— The ideal place is where you have opportunities. They're very young, and they'll get used to it and learn English fast. Once they finish College, they'll have a good level of knowledge and can get into a good university. I've lost years just studying English so I could pass the tests.

— Can you afford sustaining yourself, I mean, work and study? Isn't it too hard?

— I only work a few hours on the weekends to supplement the scholarship I get from the government. During the week, I have enough time to devote myself to studying. Besides, Flávia, here you won't have to kill yourself to support your underage children. As you are alone, you will get help for rent, which is very expensive, and other benefits for children. Here there is the concern for the well-being of the human being. You're going to have a decent life.

I didn't know there was a place I dreamed of so much. And what would it be like for my children to live away from family, friends? I thought I had everything right. I had decided in my mind, but what about them? Facing reality like that, had another weight. Joyce was getting a degree in nursing, a valued profession in England. She would certainly need to learn the language well and adapt some subjects to exercise it there. I researched, talked, dreamed, dug paths, suppressed obstacles. Gradually, everyone would adapt, and life would flow. There was no way it could go wrong.

Carlinhos sang songs with no nexus in them, invented lyrics about our lives, and, at the height of stress, when everyone was in the greatest rush in the restaurant kitchen, he would pick me up to dance and spin me in the air. I, angry, asked him to put me down, and the colleagues writhed with laughter. In a large dumpster to put cardboard boxes, he hid to scare the employees, went out to smoke without being a smoker, made bolinhos de chuva (Brazilian cinnamon doughnuts) when the boss wasn't in and communicated with all people even without speaking a word of English, only with faces and gestures. He was another Brazilian newcomer, who completely changed the environment, one more friend I made.

When winter arrived, I bought a coat, thinking it would be enough. I saw snow for the first time: I touched it, tasted it, and kneaded, making small snowballs. My winter season was associated with the time it lasted in my hometown in Brazil. There, however, it never ended. There was little sunlight. At five in the afternoon, the sky was completely dark. Those were long months. The feeling of missing everything was getting harder and harder to bear. When I was told of an issue at school or that my mom was very tired, I tried to focus on my goal. I asked the boys to collaborate because I was working hard for a better future for all of us.

There was little time left to complete a year that I had arrived in England and could not decide whether to fetch them or if I would return to Brazil. There was the possibility of entering the process of applying for Italian citizenship in Italy itself, which would be faster. However, I would need to live there for a few months, and my haste to be with them did not give me such time.

My friends encouraged me to stay another summer and raise money to sort this out. Those last two months took a while to get through. The work at the restaurant began to get too heavy; it no longer had the same enthusiasm as before. I was annoyed by the games, I didn't care if I went to work walking by the beach anymore, and everything I thought about was losing its color, sense. The distance from my kids hurt; it hurt very much.

— You're not going back to Brazil without visiting some countries in Europe, are you? You don't know if you're going to get that chance again!

— I don't have that need, Carlinhos. What I want most now is to leave.

Far from our country, our friends also became our family. They are the ones who support us when we need the most, a friendship that we will lead for the rest of our lives. They organized a farewell party in which we made plans to one day meet again.

On the way out of town, I saw the houses that had delighted me so much when I arrived — one by one cutting apart through the bus window.

Chapter 3

At the airport in Belo Horizonte, a few steps separated us. An entire orchestra played inside me. Israel was taller than the others; he had had a good growth spurt; Davi also grew up, they had the physiognomy changed by adolescence. Joyce was more beautiful, more mature, and my parents more marked by time.

I walked into the old apartment. Everything was clean and organized with affection for my return. I took a deep breath, recognizing and valuing everything I had, even the things that weren't mine. It would work out now. My strength was renewed. A special friend came to see me.

— I have a gift for you! — as she pulled a sketch from the book *Reversos* which she had beautifully illustrated and handed it to me. I didn't know how to thank her, so as I hugged her, some tears fell from my eyes.

After the euphoria of the first week, from meeting with my family and friends, I re-planned the future. The money I had saved would maintain us for the next six months. I started looking for a job, and I again had the same disappointment as before, the same feeling, the same suffering. Insecurity increased with the calendar on the kitchen wall, changing pages quickly. The advice of the Brazilian waiter began to get more frequent in my mind. I was looking for stories of families who tried a different life in other countries, especially those that worked out. One of them I came to witness years before and now served as an example. A distressed woman in the kitchen, wondering, "My God, am I doing the right thing?" She had left her four underage daughters with her mom and was trying to make a living in Canada. A year later, she was back to pick them up. The older girls, teenagers, did not want to go, wept seas of sadness hugging their boyfriends and friends. A year later, they were well adapted at school, with work and new friendships. They didn't even talk about coming back.

I wouldn't take my kids to live there illegally. That was a matter to be resolved. I went to the Italian consulate, where I was told that the long waiting time was ending. In three months, I'd be called to make the passport. The wind was in my favor, that was a good sign.

"A possible dream! Imagine, really imagine: what will our life be like, what difficulties will we face? Many! And all of them will certainly be great experiences, gains that will make us better, stronger. Joyce will join us when she finishes university. My three children together and I will be the family that we haven't been able to be until then."

The idea was consolidating and freeing me from old prisons. I talked to the boys, made plans. It was all very new, different, radical, and strange at the same time. I know they couldn't scale, but the euphoria of their friends helped them realize that it would be something very exciting because they would all like to have an opportunity like that.

I went to my parents' house to break the news and ask them once again to take care of the boys for a few months. I'd go first to get a new job and a place to live. When I was stabilized, they'd meet me in England. I knew it wasn't good news. Taking over my children for a few more months and then "losing" them to a distant country, however, is part of so many people's lives...How many would like to study abroad?

Another farewell. This time, I tried not to tear the picture. I traded the anticipated longing for the joys of close encounters and a thought-provoking future. It was a flight where there was no pain, only uncertain certainties.

Chapter 4

I arrived in Brighton on a rainy afternoon. Márcio, the Brazilian I met at Jorge and Joana's house, was also back in town. He was waiting for me at the bus stop to help with the bags. I hid under a marquee and saw him pass across the street, his clumsy way, without looking to both sides of the road. I shouted his name a few times, but he didn't listen. I had to take a cab to take me from there just three blocks away.

— Wow, what a beautiful room! — spacious, airy; the wooden furniture, the fireplace, and the windows overlooking the lanes had English elegance.

— You can have it — said Márcio. — I'm leaving for Spain in a week.

— It's too expensive, and I can't commit half my salary to rent a room.

— I'm going to talk to the owner. Maybe you can get someone to share it with.

Jorge, Joana, and their daughter had moved out. I arrived at the restaurant unannounced. Carlinhos was cleaning the hall.

— Hello! Is there anyone home?

— Oh, you *cachorra*! You didn't even tell me you were here! — we hugged, he picked me up me, started dancing, spinning me just like he used to do in the kitchen.

New employees were working there; the staff was complete; I would have to look for work elsewhere. Márcio realized that I was disheartened by the news: "There are several restaurants in the town. Get your résumé, and let's have a cup of coffee." He was like that: determined, self-assured. We entered all the cafes and restaurants from one of the main streets of the city center. He made sure of addressing the manager of each of them and introducing me. I was hired, and we had a coffee to celebrate.

The sudden change in temperature left me vulnerable. A bad flu left me in bed, and I couldn't work for about seven days. When I got back to the restaurant, the manager told me that he had to hire someone else and that this person was going to share the shift with me. She was a newly arrived Brazilian. I lost a few hours of work, but I got a friend, Leila. I went to live with her in a flat with other Brazilians.

— Girls let's throw a party on Friday? — asked Peter, the English chef, who was interested in Leila.

— Where?

— In the house where I'm renting a room. I moved in recently, people there are pretty cool. It won't be a big party: just you, the two Poles with their wives about three people from the house and me.

— Come on, Leila, let's have some fun, meet new people!

John, the head of the house, also English, polite, and attentive, got his laptop to translate a few words as we talked. We had some shots of vodka that the Poles had brought, laughed, danced, and when the living room started spinning, we took a taxi and left. I had a horrible headache the next day.

— John got worried about you, asked for your cell phone number, and I gave it to him — Peter said.

— Worried? Why?

— Because you said, you're not used to drinking vodka.

— No, not really... Hum... This concern is interesting ...

I started getting messages from John every day until we set to meet again and start dating. On Sundays, we would drive around the city surroundings. I met beautiful places, old villages, traditional pubs, antique shops, castles. He was a gentleman, always worried if I was well, serving me food, drink, filling me with affection. After all the contempt I've received in this life, I was feeling like a queen.

— Is it always going to be this way, John?

— Always — he answered with a tender look, in which I slipped and got lost.

The boys would be here in a month, and I urgently needed to rent a room for us. Whenever John saw an ad, he would call, ask for information, but when he explained that it would be for three people, two being teenagers, the owners wouldn't accept. The days went by, and my affliction increased. We'd warn every person we met until he found out about a cheap house in the suburbs of the city. It was a great rush, friends helping with shopping, cleaning, and when Israel and Davi arrived, everything was ready to receive them. We picked them up at the airport. I was a little apprehensive and wondered how they would react to my relationship with John. They were practicing some English on the way:

— John, do you like football?

— No, no, I am not a fan.

— Not possible! Manchester? Liverpool? Chelsea?

John smiled.

— No, it is not my taste. I like music. I love music!

We drove around town. Excited, I was showing and explaining everything at once. They just watched... The owner of the house had asked me to take care of his dog because they did not accept animals where he was living. I agreed immediately! It would be great for the boys to have Ringo, such an affectionate company.

I enrolled both of them in one of the best schools in town. As the school year begins in September, and we were at the end of October, we had to wait for the next cycle in December for them to start attending classes. I had got a more stable job at a big hospital in the city. I went to work early in the morning. They spent the day on the computer and didn't want to leave the house because of the cold and because they were still very insecure.

The owner came to receive the rent every week, and, at every the very first time, he told me that he had given a very low price and would need to increase it. I agreed, paid, and asked for a contract. In the third week, he increased the price again and still no contract. I didn't enjoy that situation, and I couldn't afford it. Soon there was a room at John's house, and we moved there.

— Here it will be perfect for the both of you! Just a five-minute walk from the school and the park where you can play ball and make new friends. And look at that beautiful avenue, full of trees! — I said excitedly.

— But the house is cold!

— That's true, it doesn't have a good heating system, the windows are old... Let's improvise here until things get better, OK? There's this fireplace we can use, and as soon as I can, I'll buy a wardrobe and decorate the room!

In the next room, which was also transformed into a bedroom, lived Harry, one of John's children, he had Israel's age. On the second floor, there were three bedrooms: one for John and, in the others, Peter and another Englishman.

Finally, in December, the boys began to attend school. I was blown away when I visited it. I thought I was at the wrong place. Was that a public school? It was huge, very well equipped, and very beautiful, surrounded by lawns, football and rugby fields, annexes, and connections to nearby schools.

— It looks like a university campus — Israel said.

— If there is a football field, it works for me — Davi joked about it.

Unable to disguise my anxiety, I looked out the window at the students who gathered at the bus stop or passed euphorically down the street at the end of class, trying to find Israel and Davi.

— So? How was the first day of school?

— Normal — said Israel.

— Normal — repeated Davi.

— Come on! I want to know everything!

— I didn't understand anything about the classes! — Davi confessed.

— I was super lost! I didn't know I had to change classrooms, but a girl helped me— Israel added.

— Yes, some people helped, showed me the school, stuff like that.

— A teacher called me in front of the class and asked me to show where my city was on Brazil's map.

— And during recess, some students came to try to talk to us about football. They kept saying the names of the players and the teams they know, Ronaldinho, Kaka, Robinho, Flamengo, Corinthians…

— Wow! You've had a nice day! That's cool! What about the subjects?

— We are going to have an extra lesson every day to understand the content better.

— Wow, how nice! You're going to learn quickly!

I sought out the advisor responsible for foreign students at the school to appoint me some private English teacher.

— It's going to be very expensive for you, it's not necessary. In about eight months, they will speak and understand the English language very well. Let's give them the support they need at this stage.

John, always helpful, called, asked for information, and helped me fill out forms so that Israel and Davi could continue orthodontic treatment. He also took them to meet youth football teams on the outskirts of town, trying to find some they could train in.

— You can look for the team near the house where you live, or you can try the school team — said one coach.

— On some fields that doesn't have a beam. I'm a goalkeeper, how am I going to train without a beam? — Davi complained.

It wasn't easy getting in on the school team, but soon they fitted in. They spent the whole week waiting for practice or game days, which were often canceled because of bad weather. Lots of rain, then the snow, and they wanting to play…

— Calm down, guys, when summer comes, it will all change!

When summer came, there was no training because it was the holiday season. Result: videogame.

I had seen on the school's website that they participated in sports championships in Europe, and I waited for the day that this would happen.

It would undoubtedly be a great stimulus for them, but during the years they studied there, we heard nothing about it. After five months of winter, having the computer as the only distraction, no friends, no motivation, they started talking about returning to Brazil.

— No! No! No! It's too early to think about that; you're still in the adaptation phase. By the time a year has gone by, you'll be talking and understanding the language, calm down, everything will get better. You have to leave the house, go to the park, make friends!

I saw a great difficulty in the relationship between Israel and Davi, and their distress with the English adolescents. I talked to parents, also immigrants, to advise me. I needed to understand if this situation also happened to their children, to know their experiences:

"The groups are heterogeneous, there are some who are friendly, welcoming parents, and there are those who have their restrictions on foreigners. Children repeat their parents. We have to learn to balance ourselves between these groups."

"My daughter has no friends at school. She says she's got two or three, but I don't see them. We moved here six years ago, she was seven, still little when we arrived. Her life is her family, cousins, uncles, and aunts who live here."

"It depends a lot on each one. Who is extroverted, open, doesn't have any problems, while others are more isolated. My children are different: one is more attached to the family we left behind, and it is very suffering when he spends a vacation in our country because he doesn't want to return; the other already has plans here, some friends and even girlfriend."

"Different cultures often don't mix, and I think it's best that way. I prefer my children to relate more to people in my country."

It's difficult to understand, perhaps because we are always expecting similar retribution to the way we are, to the attitudes we have. When I was a teenager, an American girl stayed a few months at one of my classmates' house for an exchange. Everyone wanted to meet her, scratch some English, be friends with her. Every day she was invited to go to someone's house and for tours on weekends. Yes, there in England, the situation was quite different: foreigners were common, and not everyone agreed with immigration policies.

As I prepared dinner, I had a conversation with Israel and Davi, who were in the kitchen:

— Don't you have any friends, someone you can hang out with, walk around the city, go to each other's homes?

— There are some that are nice, but these "ones" are friends of others who have nothing to do with it us.

I went to the school to talk to the counselor about their difficulty in adapting.

— Most of our students have known each other since elementary school. It is common to form groups, especially in this adolescence phase. Let's give it time! Next year, Israel will go to College, there will be different students, from other places in the city. At the College, there are more foreigners too, they will be more mature, it will be a new phase, and Davi will follow in his brother's footsteps.

College in the UK is professionalizing. When they finish their course, around the age of eighteen, young people have the option of going to university or falling into the job market. For most English people, living with their parents after that age is shameful — that's what I've heard many times. Maybe that's why there was a rush in John for his children's independence that there wasn't in me. He thought I needed to stay away so they could learn to get by. This was his main educational method.

Most English men can cook. There are cooking classes at school and varied cooking programs on TV, even for children. Although he knew how to, John hardly cooked, he preferred to buy his food. I, even not being skillful, did the trivial, our Brazilian food, every day. Sometimes Harry would eat too; other times, he went to the kitchen to do his experiments, leaving dirty canisters, which generated conflict, since I demanded that Israel and Davi cleaned up everything they had used. Establishing this rule with all the residents of the house was not an easy task.

On one Sunday, we made a delicious Sunday roast, a traditional English lunch, taking advantage that John's eldest son that had come to visit him. Baked potatoes, some juicy vegetables, roasted beef, and buns drizzled with meat sauce. My only requirement was rice.

—That doesn't match! — said, John.

— It does! It's perfect now!

We Brazilians don't have the habit of saying "thank you" to every request we have answered, such as receiving the glass, the spoon, the fork or the napkin, when we are in a relaxed atmosphere. As they finished their meal, John's children thanked him emphatically, which I found surprising. On the one hand, it sounded beautiful, a form of recognition, but on the other, it seemed that the father had done a great favor in feeding his children. Our lack of "thank you" was interpreted as rudeness, and lunch ended in a temper in the questioning glances.

—You know, John, — I said as I gathered the dishes from the table —, we don't usually thank all the time like you do. Often, our thanks are implicit in our attitudes and retributions. This isn't rude; it's just a different culture.

The company John worked for was in a crisis, and he was tense and irritated. There was a plan to fire several employees, and he sensed that he would be on the list. In March, on my birthday, John called Israel and Davi, handed them a few pounds, and asked them to go downtown to buy me a gift, "from the children to the mom".

— Mom, we picked this gift for you, we think it's so you!

They knew how to choose. A beautiful wooden figurine. I was moved by John's attitude and the boys' affection in choosing something special for me.

At night, I didn't want to go out; it was Saturday, I preferred to stay home and order pizzas over the phone. John gave me a very beautiful necklace of flowers and leaves, matching the earrings and the special embroidered card. Leila came to hug me, stayed with us for a few hours, but didn't want to wait for the pizza. We were all in the kitchen, watching something interesting on the computer, cheerful, relaxed when they knocked on the door. I answered it.

— It must be the pizza!

When I came back with the pizza boxes, John just started shouting words I was trying to understand amid the confusion of that scene. He was having a breakdown.

— What is going on? — I asked astonished

— You never say thank you, you don't help! — "you this, you that", words would come out of his mouth without any sense. He was completely out of himself, with his face red, shouting with no pause. Scared, I asked the boys to go to their room.

— What happened, Israel? Davi?

— Nothing! The guy just went crazy!

— Did you say something? Did something for him to be like that?

— Nothings, really nothing!

— He can't treat us this way, it's the end of our relationship...

I thought, cried, walked around. Got the present and the card he had given me hours before, walked to the kitchen and threw at his chest angrily:

— Thank you, John, now I know who you truly are!

Stunned, I called Leila. She was living at Carlinhos's house, and on that month, he was during a vacation in Brazil.

— Leila, I'm going to your house with the boys. I won't stay here any longer. I'll explain it later.

We gathered as much as we could. When we were heading out, I face John, that walked up the stairs, out of himself. Davi tried to start fighting, I stepped in front of him and asked Peter and his sister to see what was happening.

— Please, John, stop! Stop John!

We placed our things on the sidewalk. Peter offered to take us by car. His sister, a very polite Englishwoman, hugged me and apologized for John's behavior:

— Don't think all Englishmen are like that.

The next day, I called my supervisor at the hospital. She advised me to look for a government agency. I packed up all the documents they asked for, and a few days later, I was looking for a place to live. I found a nice little house that wasn't far from school, ideal for us. In a little over a month, we moved there.

During that time, I received constant messages from John, asking me to come back. I ignored them. When I went to get the rest of our belongings, he was at home and tried to talk:

— Please, get the boys and come back.

— What you did was unforgivable.

— Why is it unforgivable? Do you not know how to forgive?

I took the bags and left. The next day, he called me, asking if that was my final decision. I said, yes. I heard him crying on the other end of the line for a few seconds and hung up. I lost my way; I fell apart. A friend of his came to me, and we set up a meeting at a cafe near her house.

— Who is John?

— Flávia, John is a great man, friendly, generous… He is not violent, I've known John for years now, and he has never done anything bad to anyone. He had a breakdown; he is going through some issues, you know that.

— He asked me if we don't know how to forgive. It isn't a matter of forgiveness; I'm afraid that it will repeat itself.

— You only have to set boundaries.

— If it's a breakdown, he has no control, and it could happen again.

— Yes, and if it happens again, it will be the last time. — that's what I would do.

— Did he ask you to talk to me?

— He loves you.

— I have children; it's really hard for them to see things this way.

— If you truly love him, time can fix this and show who people truly are.

— I'm suffering too much. I didn't want to feel love, because love is a dangerous feeling.

John wasn't only generous and attentive; he also connected me with an interesting world, places, songs, people, stories. He had a special look at small things and a sharp, intelligent interpretation of others. Encouraged me for life, writing, valued what I did, my presence. Known my limitations and accepted me for who I am. Why did he destroy everything?

As I had finished my job at the hospital, I walked across the parking lot towards the street when I saw him, in front of the gate, smiling and holding a flower.

— I have something really important to talk to you.

— We don't have anything to talk about.

— Can you give me a minute?

— Say it.

— Our love is bigger than what happened. Love can change everything.

There was a sea of sincerity in those gray eyes seeking for answers on me. The idea of having a double life, a broken family, eroded me. It was just the opposite of what I was looking for. I stood there for a few seconds, drowning in unnamed justifications, seeking compensation for the incurable needs of the past, standing there, a person as imperfect as me. I became a divided person.

𝄢

The days were warmer and longer. People would lay on the lawns of the squares and on the rocks of the beach to receive the sun. And everything was cheerful and colorful without the dark, heavy winter coats. Joyce had just finished and was packing to live with us. There were very few Brazilian teenagers in Brighton. That summer, Israel and Davi met Caio and Felipe, of the same age group. Felipe seemed to be well adapted there. He was less than ten years old when he moved with his mom to England; he didn't had time to meet "the good of Brazil", as they used to say. Caio had arrived a few months ago and was going through a situation similar to that of the boys. The friendship with Caio, who was also passionate about football, was very important at that stage. They spent weekends together, went out to play ball, watched videos, movies, listened to music, played video games, exchanged school experiences. A good friend makes life possible.

𝄢

With a silk bed sheet of flowers and a sky-blue curtain, I prepared her room with garden airs. The house, quite old, but pleasant, had a large room with a fireplace, where I put photos and plants. The three bedrooms and bathrooms were upstairs, as all traditional English houses. We took the bushes out of the backyard, discovering the glass greenhouse. There was also an apple tree and a cherry tree, which looked wonderful at that season. In another tree, shy, I hung a tree fern fiber with colorful flowers, and, on the door, I placed a large vase with white petunias. Joyce arrived, bringing the missing sister and daughter into our family, and we resumed our story.

In the morning, she took an English course and, in the late afternoon, worked in the same hospital as me, serving meals to patients. Soon she got to know a group of Brazilians. They were always meeting, and the atmosphere of the house changed. There were parties, joy, chicken *coxinha*, and sweets that she liked to make for her brothers.

— We're missing a dog in this house! — they would say.

It was sad when we had to return Ringo. In Brazil, several dogs went through our lives, but it was never possible to keep any of them because the conditions were always unfavorable. We had to donate them, and I comforted the boys by saying that if we ever lived in a house with a backyard, we'd have a dog. Well, we were living in one now, and the conditions were favorable. Dogs are joy, companionship, and a path to socialization. Taking him to the park every day for a walk, leaving home, meeting other people with the same interests, all sounded like a great idea. At school, Israel commented on this desire with a classmate, who took him to a kennel where animals are kept for adoption. Joyce took the lead, exciting everyone, making plans, solving issues. After two weeks, with all the procedures required by the kennel fulfilled — which was not as simple as we thought— we finally took Fred home, a beautiful Belgian shepherd, half-breed, black and fearful. As much as the boys tried, he became fonder of me and Joyce, revealing some trauma to males. When the boys took him for a walk, he refused, forcing his way back. It was like this for a long time, with some little progress.

The following year, Israel went to College, where he began the fitness course he wanted so badly. Davi did not know what subjects to choose beyond those obligatory. I tried to encourage him to design classes. As a child, he loved to draw, he was very creative, he had a special gift, but in the first few weeks he was disappointed it wasn't what he wanted. He hadn't drawn in a long time, it seemed as it was only a childhood phase. As time had gone by to change the course, he had to continue until the end of the cycle. Maybe, to make up for the dissatisfaction, he decided to work. He was fourteen, and it wasn't easy to get a job at that age. With school hours that needed which to be accomplished, from 8:45 a.m. until 3:15 p.m., the options were minimal. The law in the UK doesn't allow under-18s to work in places that sell alcoholic beverages, and other shops closed at five in the afternoon. What remains for this age group is delivering newspapers from home to home, about an hour before or after school. Determined, he sought out the newspaper agency closest home. He came back happy; he had got his first job. There was only room for the morning shift. He'd wake up at six o'clock, go to the agency, pick up the bag full of newspapers and the route of the day. He would come home, eat breakfast, put on his uniform, and go to school. There was no day off; it was from Monday through Monday, which compromised his weekend. The pay was derisory. I thought it was an exploitation of minors, I didn't agree, but he didn't care, he did it with discipline: went to bed early, got up without having to call him and was happy when he got paid on Saturdays. He saved money and liked to buy his things, pay for his bus fare, his snack, his clothes. On the other hand, he saw me giving Israel money to do the same things and didn't like it.

— Israel doesn't work, and you give everything to him!

— Davi, save your money! The same things I give Israel, I give it to you. Create your savings account, save your money from work.

But the pleasure he had on paying for his expenses was great, he felt very well by doing it.

When winter tightened, Davi became ill, had a very strong flu. Still, he didn't want to stop working. He would come back coughing, his face red of cold, and would go straight to bed. Christmas was good for him, he won thank you cards from customers with beautiful messages of appreciation and good tips. When he got sick again, I didn't let him go on. I went to the news agency to report that he wasn't in good health. The owner complained by showing me the pile of newspapers on the floor. I didn't like that lack of concern for the health of the exploited employee, so I said he had a better look for someone else to do the job because Davi wouldn't return. I comforted Davi by saying we'd get a better job, but we didn't get anything. I went to the support center for young people and adolescents in the region, where they support only those who are out of school. I tried to explain that my son had a lot of idle time at home, that he was looking for a job, and he couldn't find it. It didn't do any good.

Too cold and not much sunlight... A few months after Joyce's arrival and friendship with Caio, life became difficult and dull again. What was positive wasn't enough to fill the absence they felt of their old friendships, of their homeland. Israel and Davi began to press me again to return to Brazil. I needed to be firm, or they would waste the best opportunity of their lives. I know that at that age it is difficult for many to program the future, life is quite immediate, what matters is "here and now". I could understand them because I was also like that, but there was a much greater goal that wasn't far from being achieved. We searched the internet for indoor soccer teams since field soccer practices weren't so frequent. We didn't find anything in Brighton, just in other distant cities. We contacted a professional team of Brazilians in London. The training days were different for Israel and Davi because of their age group. I wasn't in a position to take them, and they were too young to go alone. In addition, the distance and time they would spend on the route made the idea unfeasible.

— Why don't we move to London? It would be much easier, wouldn't it? — they insisted.

—It's not that simple. I have a job here.

— There are hospitals there.

— Over there, everything is distant and expensive. You need to take the underground all the time, I get distressed just from thinking about it. It's much easier to live here! Everything is close, the city is airy, and we have this house close to your school…

Davi, blunt as always, tireless, was planning our moving. As he liked to be a goalkeeper, in indoor football he would have more chances because of his stature. I believed that over time the right opportunities would arise for them.

That year, Joyce and I decorated the house for Christmas and prepared a special dinner. We didn't go to our friends' house because on that day there is no transport, no buses or taxis. We called our relatives in Brazil. The boys went to bed early. No fun. Caio didn't have any friends at school either. I was worried and sad for them. My adolescence was made up of parties, meetings in the homes of colleagues, meetings for schoolwork, weekend outings, shopping malls, cinema, club, disco, first dates — everything was exciting and full of life. When would that situation get better? Joining College made no difference to Israel. Would it be when they got a girlfriend? At one point, love happens...

I entered the new year renewing my hopes, without fear of it working out. We heard of a boxing gym not far from home, where Davi began training. At that time, he watched several quite often the videos of Rocky Balboa that Joyce had given him as a gift. He was a card-carrying fan of the persistent, dedicated character, who knew where he wanted to go and the beatings he would have to take.

Several times a day, I would look at the silver Vectra through my bedroom window to shake me with contentment. When could I have a car in Brazil living as I did? It was a used and cheap car but able to give the city another dimension. Joyce and I would take, and pick up the boys at places, the way between the house and the job was done in minutes and going to the supermarket was much less stressful.

I was very grateful to England and my Italian ancestors for being part of the European Community. This is what all countries should do for their citizens, and not leave them to a minimum, without jobs, opportunities, quality education, quality medical care, watching the favelas grow, and violence increasing.

Chapter 5

About a year after we were living in that house, I received a letter from the owner telling me that he had to put it up for sale and that we would have two months to leave it. A few hours later, I got a call from my mom:

— Daughter, we bought the ticket! Your father, your aunt and I will arrive in two months, we will stay for twenty days!

Later, when they arrived from school, Israel and Davi came to tell me determinedly:

— Mom, we can't adapt here. This is YOUR dream, not ours. We want to go back to Brazil.

I took a deep breath...

— My dear children, it's May. It's one month to the end of the school year. I'll buy the tickets for you to go to Brazil ON VACATION. Spend two months there. Walk around, meet your friends, have fun and then come back at the end of August, renewed and prepared for the beginning of classes in September, agreed?

— But buy us the ticket back for the 4th of September, because classes don't start until the 5th.

One less problem to worry about. I started a long journey looking for a house to rent. After a month, I knew all the advertisements that existed in the city, but there was always some obstacle: some houses were very far from the school, some owners did not accept dogs, others did not admit teenagers, others did not approve my rent. Passing through a neighborhood at the entrance of the city, John saw an ad they had just placed. He called immediately and made an appointment to visit. This time, it worked. The next day, I signed the contract. The house was very good, spacious, with a huge yard for Fred and near the school. It couldn't be better! It was a week before my parents, and my aunt arrived when we moved in. Joyce and I arranged everything the best way, but we still didn't have time to buy curtains and some furniture. One night while we were having dinner, my parents asked:

— So, Joyce, what are your plans? Are you going to be a nurse at Brighton Hospital?

— No... I'm not going to be here much longer. It would take me years to get that, and I already think I'll come back. I just want to finish the English course I'm taking, and at the beginning of next year, I'll definitely go back to Brazil.

After fourteen months in England, she was in a better position to evaluate her life and where she wanted to put it.

— I don't see myself living here. I want to be close to my grandparents, who are getting older — she told me later when I asked her if she was sure of her decision.

I wanted to be family, to be structure, to be ground, and I couldn't do it. I stood there, watching my road break again.

On the trails in the park, I walked with Fred every afternoon before going to work. It was the same big park as before, only we were living on the other side now, and the landscape was different. You could see the sea from the top of the golf course and the hills on the other side, turning yellow with the flowers of the season. There, I had moments of paradise. When I was off duty, John would sometimes surprise me by bringing a cup of coffee and Fred a bone.

— Did you write any poems today?

— It was just a phase, John. It's over now.

— Why don't you believe in yourself? Why do you hide them? I like your poems; like me, other people will too. I want a poem as a gift! Promise?

I chose some dry leaves from the trees in my collection, kept in the newspapers in the backyard, and I made a picture for him, with frames that I bought in the little charity shops, and they were piling up in a corner.

— That's all I got, that's all I got.

We used to meet on Saturdays. There was no more contact between him and the boys. It would still take time to sew up that torn road.

𝄢

In two months in Brazil, Israel and Davi lived everything they had not done in two years in England: excited friends from everywhere, parties, tours, trips, beach, joy. My plan had gone wrong. They came back even more convinced that that was where they wanted to stay.

— Did you like the new house? Isn't it big? Much better than the other one! Near the school, the neighborhood is great, everything is perfect! Another school year was beginning, new friends, it'll be different, for sure!

I was trying to keep positive expectations, but it was hard. On that vacation in Brazil, Davi met Bia, his first girlfriend. In love, they needed to breathe the same air. They talked for hours on the internet, exchanged letters, cards, and all the forms they could find to express that love with no size. A month after classes started, Israel asked me to talk:

— Mom, I recognize all your efforts to bring us to England, all your concern for our future... I tried, Mom, but I'm not happy here. I want to go back. Don't worry, I'll manage to turn around — and hugged me, and his hug shut me.

𝄢

I had already adopted Caio as "my weekend son." Every Friday, he would go straight from College to our house and only leave Sunday night on the last bus. He was full of plans, contagious happiness, he looked famous in the selfies and rehearsed interviews for after the victorious games: he had just passed a test for an English football team and would soon start training.

— Really?! That's wonderful, Caio! That's all you wanted! I'm so happy for you!

He was ecstatic, and it was days in that crazy euphoria, games, and future projects. The right opportunities would come to each one at the right time.

We hadn't talked about his return yet when Israel told me he was invited to a party in Coventry.

— Coventry? Where is it?

—It's beyond London, about a three-hour drive from here.

—Wow, what a far-off party. Who are the people?

— It's the birthday of a girl I met on Facebook.

— Brazilian? English? Indian?

— Brazilian.

— But it's too far for you to go and come back on the same day.

— She said I could sleep there, she's already talked to her mom, it's all sorted.

— Fine, go! Go have fun, meet new people!

Israel came back dating. He went to Coventry almost every weekend and never talked about going back to Brazil. He and Bel were happy, and my hope that a relationship would bring a bit of sunshine was being confirmed.

On the other hand, Davi was apathetic, totally uninterested in his studies. The productivity had dropped a lot. He was quiet and sad. I was called the school, which told me that they tried to talk to Davi, but he said it was all right, that he would solve his problems himself.

— The adaptation for them here is very difficult, they don't want to stay, even more now that Davi has come back from Brazil dating.

— Let's wait for that phase to pass, what happened to his brother will happen to him, and then things will change. But try to make him understand that he needs to work hard and keep studying.

Yes, things were changing, but for the worse. He started missing a lot of class. I had to call the school every time and justify it. It's the parents' obligation to do that.

— Davi, you're going to miss the year if you keep doing this!

He didn't care. One morning, I walked into his room and made him dress his uniform.

— Finish the course, Davi! Don't delay your life! It'll be worse for you!

He put on his uniform, but in the kitchen, he said he wouldn't go to school. I pushed him out and locked the door from the inside. He was depressed, and even though I'd been through it, I couldn't deal with it. I looked out the window and saw him sitting in the garden, in the cold, in the snow, without a hat, without gloves. I opened the door and called him to talk.

— Let's settle this another way, Davi, but please don't leave school.

— I can't stand staying here anymore.

— Davi, everything passes in life... I know it's hard for you to understand, first love is very strong, but it's not the only one. You will meet other people, you will love other people, but if you have to stay together one day, you will, life brings you back.

I told the story of the passionate couple who suffered so much from the separation when the girl went to live in United Studies. A few months later, each had already found a new love and life was moving on. And the story of the boy who came to Brighton, broke off his engagement because the girl didn't want to come. A few years later, they met again and got married.

— Look at your brother: couldn't even imagine meeting someone here... It'll happen to you too!

It was no use, Davi dragged himself through life, without any motivation.

I was suffering too, frozen road.

𝄢

Joyce bought her ticket.

— I enrolled in a post-graduation course in Brazil. I will have arrived there on a Saturday, and classes start on Monday — she said with her eyes shining and her expectations coloring her face.

A few days before her trip, I drove by the park and saw her playing with Fred. I slowed down, stopped, and watched from afar. My heart tightened, and I cried. *"But it was all either surpassed or not enough."* I kept the verses that Álvaro de Campos wrote in *Passagem das Horas*.

During the time she stayed in Brighton, we had some arguments. She needed to break everything that was badly built between the two of us, collect all the pieces that were missing in her life that I didn't know how to fill, cry all the sorrow that had accumulated in a very beautiful and serene lake, but that was actually a river that needed to flow. An uncomfortable emptiness settled between us. We would have to plant some flowers in these open spaces with our pain in order to heal it. She was the one who told me when saying goodbye at the station: "Don't worry, Mom, things will get better with the distance".

"One day, you will return to your country. People have roots too," a friend told me years ago. I didn't give it much thought. I'm a plant that adapts to different circumstances, as long as they don't kill me. My country was killing me. I left there dry, without leaves.

I was walking around the backyard in the last house I lived in Brighton looking for something I could save. They were going to pass a tractor the next day, removing everything for a renovation. I saw a plant among rocks. I pulled it out carefully so it wouldn't hurt its roots. "If between rocks and this suffocating bush you can survive so beautifully, imagine in this big pot, all yours, with fertile soil, how wonderful it will look!" I put the vase in front of the house, where the morning sun beats down. A few days later, she died. I was sad, I felt guilty for taking her from the place where she was so well, even having almost nothing.

Davi kept asking me to let him go.

— Son, the support I can offer is here. It's to give you the structure to study until you're independent and move on with your lives the way you want.

— We can't live in this country. Joyce is gone, Israel, if he doesn't stay with his girlfriend, he will too. We can't, Mom. You have to understand, we can't.

— Look, Davi, I could say, "OK, let's all go back to Brazil, only I'm too scared of not being able to take care for you again. You're sixteen, I wanted you finish at least College, but if you can't live here, then talk to your father, stay with him now, because your grandparents have done so much for us. I need to keep working here because this is where I can tell my children "count on me".

Davi understood, got it right with his father, and in March, I took him to the airport. Life entered him willingly. He had the excitement of a player about to take the field, a little nervous about the announcements on the speaker, the fear of missing the flight. His hug was quick — he had a lot of things to hug on the way, while mine wasn't finished yet.

His rehabilitation was surprising. In Brazil, he went back to what he naturally was. He was elected head of the class in the first weeks of school and joined the football team at school, where he met some child-hood friends again. Bia was there, like a sunflower.

Israel was still studying and dating Bel, the girl from Coventry. That relationship held them both there because she was also rootless. She didn't tear up her European passport like her friend did, but when the situation became unbearable with her stepfather, she threw everything up and went to Brighton.

My communication with Davi was not frequent because he had no Internet. He lived between his grandma's house and my parents' apartment. He didn't have a fixed place. One day I called my mom, he was there.

— Davi, you need a laptop. I'll give you an early birthday present so you can do your schoolwork and we'll be in touch.

— Not now, wait a few days.

— Wait a few days. Why?

— Just wait a few days.

He didn't want to say why. I imagined several hypostases, and I thought someone was already providing one. The next time we talked, I insisted on the present.

— That won't be necessary, Mom, I'm going back to England.

— What? This's a joke, isn't it? — I tried to detect on his voice a hidden laugh, ready to burst. I couldn't find it.

— It's true.

— What do you mean? What's going on? Are you crazy?

— Bia's father was transferred to São Paulo. They're moving.

— But you're happy there at school with your friends, aren't you? Why don't you stay? You can go to São Paulo occasionally, and she, to Belo Horizonte. Here is much further from São Paulo.

I was confused and surprised at myself, encouraging him to stay in Brazil.

— I have no home here, Mom. I have no place to live.

— But aren't you at your father's grandma's house?

— Mom, I don't feel well anywhere. I don't want to talk about it. I want to go back to College.

I wondered how he felt lost and under pressure. He should hear criticism everywhere he went about his decision to trade England for Brazil from people who probably never lived outside their country, which can only see the wonderful things. Now I had to resolve this conflict. If in Brazil Davi had no place to stay, here was his home, his room, his space, his freedom, his laundry, his noodles, his brother, his mom, and our dog. Every experience brings maturity. May he come back with new perspectives! He sold his Xbox to pay for the ticket, and there we went, once again, starting over.

Life there is really a coming and going. Caio returned with his family to Brazil. He left the football team behind. He believed he'd have good chances anywhere. For some, I dream, for others, an illusion. It's hard to live reality. Davi became friends with Bel, his brother's girlfriend. They went to the same school, the same gym, watched funny videos on the internet, listened to music — it was a very good phase for the three of them.

When Israel turned eighteen, he began working in a large restaurant downtown Brighton. Excited about his first job and earning his own money, he decided to leave school for the next semester.

𝄢

The drawings of armed policemen, shooting, the bullets going through the sheet of paper, hitting outsiders, drew attention by the firm strokes, by the perspective, by the absorbed state in which he stayed while unloading what he had in mind. With crayons, Davi, at the age of five, reconstructed violent images of the world around him. It's a good thing there were so many pages with birds and footballs.

— I enrolled in the Public Services course! — he said as he walked into the house, excited, throwing his backpack into a corner — I'm going to be a cop!

He identified with strong, determined people. In the "Captain Nascimento" phase, Davi incorporated the character from the movie Elite Squad: he would come down the stairs of the house with his arms stretched out, as if he were holding a gun, shouting: "Everybody lie down! On the ground! On the ground!", really wanting us to do the scene, elbowing me to obey the order while I was cooking. He was repeating lines that he memorized in the middle of our conversations with the imposing and authoritarian voice of a military man:

— 'Zero Five'! Pass the salad, please! 'Do you hear me, Zero Five?'

— Davi, today is your day to clean the yard — I reminded him of your task.

— 'Mrs. Flávia 'mission given, mission accomplished!'

— I'm very tired, I'm not going to the academy today... — mumbled Bel.

— 'Can't stand it? Ask to leave! Ask to leave!'

— Did you like the movie, Davi? — asked Israel.

— 'Knife in the skull'!

In the second week, he complained that the course was too slow and dull.

— Relax, Davi, you have to learn the theory first.

Days later, he arrived home telling us that he finally had a good class: "The teacher took us to that lagoon in Hove where water sports are practiced and divided the class into two groups that would compete with each other for some physical activities. After several races, the two groups were tied! Very exciting! The final race would be decisive! Each group got on a boat, and the teacher warned that whoever caught the ball would be victorious and threw the ball in the middle of the lagoon! It was very crazy! Everyone paddled with their hands, shouting, only it would go away when we got close, then I couldn't stand it! When I saw that the other group was almost making it, I jumped into that icy water in my clothes and caught the ball! The other group didn't want to accept, said it wasn't worth it, but the teacher praised my attitude. That's how I gave the victory to my group! I'm the guy! I'm the guy!

He really engaged on the things he did. I couldn't believe it when he dropped out.

— I can't pursue the police career here in England. It's just for people with British passports.

— But you can do it, let's find out how it works.

— I've already got informed: I have to be of legal age and have the intention to reside definitively in the United Kingdom, I don't.

— But you can do other services within the corporation, can't you?

— What I want, I can't.

Discouraged, he attended classes just so he wouldn't miss the year but listening to Brazilian rap his dream of becoming a policeman was falling apart. The corrosive lyrics denounced the submission, the misery of thousands of people living under an annihilating system, showing violent police, often unfair and cruel. To try to resolve this great conflict, Davi spent days researching the Internet. He wanted, at all costs, to promote a meeting, a face to face debate with his idols of the moment, *Mano Brown*, rapper of the group *Racionais MC's*, and the ex-military *Rodrigo Pimentel*, one of the authors of the book *Tropa de Elite*.

"Mom, sit here, look at this interview I've found", "Watch this video!", "Pay attention to the lyrics of this song!", "I want to put them both face-to-face! Wow... it's going to be so cool! I want to see how one will disarm the other! But how am I'm going to get that? Do you think they'll pay attention to a seventeen-year-old boy?", were the things he said with excitement. He found the idea bold and very interesting.

— Try. If you don't try, you won't know.

— I got to go over there, talk to the guys, organize the stuff...

— Impossible. Try other way. E-mailing, it's cheaper.

Davi was so interested in understanding social relations, the role of politics, religion in the formation of society, that he thought about studying sociology. He cooked his brains out until he gave up the debate and started again a tireless search for a job. Every day he went out delivering resumés in stores, in companies, everywhere possible. His expectation was so great that caused him an enormous frustration with the answers that did not happen.

— Patience, Davi! When you turn eighteen, the doors will open, everything will improve. Soon enough!

I was trying to comfort him on one side, while watching all that energy wasted on the other by a limiting system, which imposes the same rules on everyone, a trainer of repeaters, which doesn't take into account the individualities, doesn't let the creative create, the expansive expand. Whoever doesn't fit in, will probably have to live on luck. And if it fits, it could be something so asphyxiating, capable of making people's souls sick.

— If insurance wasn't so absurd in this country, I could learn how to drive, pick up a truck, deliver some loads across Europe... Why is insurance here so expensive? It's only after twenty-six years old is it payable? Why do young people cause accidents? It means that the young guy, good driver, cautious has no chance! Just because he's young, they think he's irresponsible, don't they?

He complained, complained and went to the computer to make his virtual trips on video games.

— Mom, are we watching *Carga Pesada* today?

— We've seen that chapter three times!

— No, this is another one! Look at the road, what a thrill! Wow! It's crazy, look! It's crazy man! It's really crazy!

One day, Davi ran down the stairs, screaming:

— I got a job! I got a job!

— Did you? Where?

— In a restaurant! I guess they didn't care at my age. I'm gonna get it, I'm gonna get it! Lend me some shoes Israel! Are these pants okay? Hand me that shirt, Mom!

Two hours later, he was back.

— What happened, Davi?

— They didn't see my age... I started to work, the manager, the super good guy, taught me the job, then they called me at the office saying I couldn't work there because of my age, they hadn't seen it when I handed in the resume that I was only seventeen. Nobody was ever admitted and fired in such a short time!

This time, he laughed at the situation, took it in jest. I thought he was fine, but deep down, he wasn't. He went into a rebellious phase, throwing all the frustration on me. He, who often tried to make his sister understand my position, my crooked ways, was now there to charge me for the mom I couldn't be, the wife, the daughter, all at once. We argued when he came with sharp words. It's not easy to control yourself at those moments, so I would show him my calloused hands and say that I only had the responsibility to him until he was eighteen.

One afternoon, I went off to work totally desolate.

— When will that pass? — I'd get off my chest with a friend.

— It's hard when we're not recognized for our accomplishments, our attempts, when they don't understand our weaknesses, and don't forgive our mistakes. You know, young people are very radical, full of pain, of charges. Don't be shaken, it's just a phase, you'll see!

When I finished my shift at the hospital while changing clothes to leave, I got a call from him:

— Mom, can you pick me up? I'm at the bus stop in front of the school.

— All right, fifteen minutes.

He got in the car, and in an authoritarian way he inherited from police movies, he said:

— Turn right, there in front, make the turn on the avenue.

— May I ask what for?

— Take me to John's house.

— What for? — I asked stunned. That didn't make any sense. They haven't met since that terrible day of my birthday three years ago. The boys knew we were together. At first, they didn't agree, but after seeing so many kind and generous attitudes from John towards me, they ended up accepting, but without any attempt to approach.

— Davi, may I know your intentions?

— Trust me. Take me to John's house.

I stopped the car in front of the flat and went inside to call him.

— Davi's outside. He wants to talk to you.

He's got his body in awe.

— What does he want?

— I don't know.

John put on his robe and went to the sidewalk. Davi was still in the car.

— Hello, John.

— Hello, Davi.

Davi reached out his hand in a gesture of friendship. John gave a typical, playful laugh, corresponding to the gesture by shaking Davi's hand.

— Friends? — asked Davi.

— Friends! — replied John.

They exchanged a few more words, planned to meet soon to talk and we left.

— Thank you, son, your attitude was very worthy.

He really wanted to surprise me. Bel told me later that Davi was feeling very bad after our discussion and wanted to do something to redeem himself.

On August 10th, 2013, Davi turned eighteen. Soon after, he was called to fill a vacancy in the same restaurant where Israel worked. He entered a new phase, competitive and full of challenges. He wanted to embrace everything at once and was bitter with himself when he made a mistake. He overcharged himself.

— It's normal to make mistakes, son, you're learning.

— How was it with you? What did you do wrong? How did your boss take it?

The tension was huge or them, beginners, because in that restaurant they only hired people with experience, and they didn't, they lied to get the job. Little by little, they were overcoming the difficulties with the help of their friends.

The interests no longer coincided, and the outdated words they exchanged were just another sign that the lives of Israel and Bel would take different directions. It did not take long for her to decide to return to Brazil. I insisted that Israel do one more module of their course in London even though his sadness at the end of the relationship made the grey days of England even heavier, harder to breathe. At the age of twenty, owner of his money, he would now follow his own life. He bought his ticket for there a few months later, at the end of the year. This time, I thought it best not to interfere with where he would stay. He would go back to my parents' house.

It looks like it imitates, it looks like it repeats. Sometimes all is taken, and suddenly a flower is given. That's life: strange. Now it was Davi's turn to travel on his days off to see his girlfriend, a Brazilian girl he also met on Facebook. It was nice to see the two of them going out on a clear day for a walk on the beach when she came to visit him. He, full of expectations, between winds and gales would discover his paths.

Leo had an engaging conversation, a serious way that imposed respect and, at the same time, relaxed, a mixture that gave him an unusual characteristic. Two months before Israel left, he and Davi got to know this twenty-one-year-old Spaniard. Leo had just arrived in the city and was working part-time as a delivery man. He had a lot of ideas, he liked the commercial area, doing business, I thought it would be great for Israel and Davi to relate to a person like that. Since they had no plans to go to university, I had been encouraging them both to do market research, business, investments so that they would have alternatives.

Davi made calculations and more calculations analyzing costs, expenses, in which it would be possible to save, invest. What seemed to be a positive and conscious attitude was for him a cause of suffering, anxiety, excessive concern about the present and the future. Israel, on the other hand, was looking for ways to live that did not demand of him what he was not prepared to give without caring about judgments. "Mild" was his favorite word.

The money Leo received as a delivery man was very little: he paid the rent for a room and the expenses for the car, and what was left over was barely enough to eat. I offered him garden services in exchange for meals until he got a better job. When the free time coincided, the three of them would drive out for a walk on the outskirts of town. I found out later that, in one of those outings, Leo introduced Israel and Davi to his great friend, marijuana. I knew that this was possible to happen one day, as it happened to me and to so many people in their youth. My children were athletes, they lived in the gym. That didn't suit them, it was just an experience, that's what I thought.

With persuasive speech, Leo tried to confirm the veracity of his words by showing on the internet the benefits of marijuana, its medicinal and therapeutic use being increasingly adhered to in certain treatments in several countries. Fairy for some, monster for others. I lived with people who worked only to feed their addiction, who could not invest in the future, wasting their lives and good opportunities, and I saw people with affected brain, living out of reality after several years using this herb "harmless, natural and beneficial", as advocated Leo. These were the saddest and most compromising cases that I focused on in my conversations with Israel and Davi. The big issue was not to forbid them, but to convince them that it was not worth it.

Davi started driving school. Wouldn't wait eight years to pay less expensive insurance. Now he had his own money and could invest in his dreams. If on one hand he was free from that phase of long waiting and frustrations of his adolescence, on the other he was overly apprehensive about the future. After a difficult climb, when he reached the top of the mountain, he saw many others ahead of him.

Nothing is permanent in this life. I hadn't learned my lesson yet. Israel was packing.

— One thing was missing, Israel.

— What?

— You didn't rebel against me or the world.

— It's because you had a peaceful pregnancy when I was in your belly. That's why.

— It makes sense... Joyce and Davi came in times full of turbulence and uncertainty... Enjoy the experience of those five years you lived here, son, the language you learned, the school, work, the places you knew, everything, everything that happened, the good and the bad things. They make you stronger — I said during our farewell at the airport. I threw good thoughts into his path and tried to hold back the cry. Me, flooded road.

On the day of the driving test, I took Davi to Worthing, about thirty minutes from Brighton, where the test was scheduled. He didn't want to go in the instructor's car, as was conventional. He had a peculiar way of doing things, like following his intuition. We left home early; he'd have to report at eight in the morning. He was focused, avoided talking on the way. While I was having coffee on the corner, I saw him leave the parking lot driving the red car. He came back forty-five minutes later without a smile. He made a mistake that disqualified him.

On the way back home, he relaxed, and we started talking about Leo, who lately was revealing other characteristics of his personality that I didn't like. Davi wanted to convince me that I was wrong.

— Davi, my body is tense, I haven't slept well, I'm overwhelmed with problems. Please, I cannot discuss this with you now! — I said almost crying. I was really stressed out.

— Calm down, calm down, Mrs. Flávia, relax... — he said by making stroking my head. — Ninety percent of our concerns are unnecessary. "Pre-occupation" means early suffering from a situation that doesn't exist. Ninety percent of what you suffer is for nothing!

I loved it when he came in with these clever conversations. I stopped the car in front of the house.

— You're going for a ride with Fred now? — he asked.

— No. Look at the storm that's setting...

— Let's go for a quick walk on the golf course. I want to talk to you.

A few days earlier, I was shocked to see Leo wearing a jacket Davi had given him as a gift. I went to his room to ask for an explanation.

— Davi, what does that mean?

— I gave it to him as a gift.

— I gave this jacket as a gift to you, that's a huge snub, not just for material value, but sentimental. Do you remember how much you wanted that jacket?

— The guy's a partner. It was a way to show my friendship.

That boy's sure-fire way of putting his observant and critical opinion was impressing Davi. Leo really had a strong position, only he didn't know how to use it. He wanted to show his cunning, wisdom, his reason even over the rules of my house, disallowing me. He ignored my request not to smoke inside the house, accidentally burning the carpet. He threw away some reminders that I left in the kitchen, saying that nobody there needed it. When he crashed his car, it didn't take long to buy another one. I thought he had recovered too quickly, that his work was much better. I found out later that he was still at the same part-time job and that he bought the car with money he borrowed from Israel and Davi, who worked hard in the restaurant. I couldn't stand the friendship between them any longer.

Davi and I talked on the golf course until the words couldn't explain by themselves our opposing ideas about Leo and we raised the tone, thinking that then, they would change meaning or become stronger. We fought tensely in the middle of the wind and the dark, low clouds.

— So, you won't talk to him? — he asked.

— I have nothing to talk to him about, I don't want him in my house anymore. He has crossed the line.

— You don't know how to give in, you don't know how to admit you're wrong, you never knew!

— I don't have to give in. You can't see things the way they are!

— What things the way they are? The way they are in your head, just in your head! Is that your final word?

— Yes!

He turned around and walked away with heavy footsteps. I walked on the opposite direction. I felt that Davi was breaking some bond in our relationship. I couldn't lose him to that boy and marijuana. I turned around and walked out screaming his name in the middle of the storm. I couldn't find him. When I got home, I saw his wet sneakers in the lobby, he was already in his room, the door closed. "That'll pass..." I thought.

We couldn't afford to stay in that house just me and Davi. We had been living under this strain since Joyce and Israel decided to leave. An uncle of John's had an old house in town, locked up. He wanted to renovate it and sell it, but he would need time to raise the money. He asked us if we wanted to rent it the way it was, until everything worked out. We went to see the property, I, discouraged, did not want to live in the old house, they are very cold, and the bathrooms are usually awful. However, it wouldn't hurt to take a look.

— The house is big, it has room for me, for you, for Davi and for Fred.

It was dirty, dark, full of cobwebs, holes on the ceiling and on some walls. The windows were new, good, double-glazed. One of the rooms next to the kitchen was good, with thick pieces of wood on the ceiling and a fireplace that made the place cozy. Some rooms were bad, musty, others not so bad. The bathroom, to my surprise, was large and very presentable. I talked to Davi about this possibility. John and I would pay the expenses and he could save all his money. He got thoughtful. That approach years ago never really happened; it was just that handshake.

I called Davi to see the big house, he wouldn't. The contract was expiring, I had to deliver the house and started packing our things.

— Davi, we can do things differently this time. Think about it.

Days later I heard him talking to a friend on his cell phone saying that he had made up his mind to go with us to the big house.

Chapter 6

John was also delivering the small flat in which he lived alone. His son Harry had left home for over a year, worked, and lived with friends. We were exhausted by so many comings and goings in our spare time. Davi wasn't helping. The house we lived in was almost empty, and he kept going back there after work.

— Davi, there is no fridge there, what are you going to eat?

— I bought pizza.

— Come, Davi, we're waiting for you! — left messages, but he didn't respond. He was sleeping a lot; it was another depression crisis.

One afternoon, around six o'clock, he knocked on the door of the big house. I saw him from the window, and I was elated to receive him. John accompanied me, wanted to be the first to receive Davi, opened the door, and, before any word, made a sign to him pointing out the two stone lions, one on either side of the entrance. Davi smiled, understanding the joke. He and John are Leo sign.

— Welcome Davi, come in, choose your bedroom! — said John.

We had very nice evenings talking, listening to music, making food, drinking beer. We planned to have a family Christmas. John called his two sons, set up the tree, made a special dinner. One of the boys called to tell me he wasn't going that night, and the other one didn't show up. Davi went up to his room, barely touched the food. He had refused to spend Christmas with friends at the restaurant to stay with us.

— I'll take you to their house, it's still early — I offered.

— No, I didn't pay for the part of the expense of the party...

— No one is going to care about that, you can take something, it was unforeseen, they'll understand.

— I'm going to bed. Goodnight.

The excitement from the first few days in the house passed. He didn't participate so much in the conversations with John, avoiding him a few times, staying more in his room. Every once in a while, he'd meet Leo, see them both out the window, driving out. Meanwhile, downstairs the mood was festive. John, passionate about music, always received a visit from some friends.

We were gradually improving the appearance of the house: we painted doors, walls, put curtains, and it was getting more pleasant. Davi was still distant. He spent hours on Skype, talking to his father in Brazil. One of these times, he decided to have a meeting, me, him, and his father, to settle past issues. He asked me insistently, as he did when he wanted to achieve a goal.

— Davi, I don't have anything to say, discussing things from the past makes no sense.

— You don't want to dialogue because you know you're wrong. You can't face reality.

— It's not that... I don't believe we should rummage, looking for who is guilty. I'm in a different phase of life.

— If you don't have anything to fear, sit down, and talk. Can you do that? Sit down and talk?

— Fine Davi. Fine. Let's do it.

I set down, in front of the computer, his father was on the screen.

— Everything okay, Mrs. Flávia?

— Yes, and you?

Davi started:

— I've talked to my father; we want a round table with the whole family to solve our past issues. We are going to clear everything up, see who is right, who is wrong.

— That's ridiculous! I won't submit myself to that! What you are thinking is ridiculous

— I stood up outraged and left the room, going down the stairs under Davi's protests.

— Do you see it, Mom? You can't handle it! You can't face it! You hide, don't admit, Mom!

— I won't submit myself to an inquisition, Davi, I don't need to prove anything to no one, life shows it. Not words, but actions show who people truly are.

— If you don't have anything to fear, then why won't you face it? Can you see it?

I walked in the kitchen, stunned. John was there, trying to listen, understand what was happening:

— Why didn't you talk to your ex-husband?

— They want a family debate, an inquisition! This is ridiculous!

— Davi wants to listen to both sides of your past relationships, yours and his fathers. He wants to take his own conclusions.

— Like that? Making a public judgment? I won't submit myself to that!

— Not accepting it makes you look guilty of something.

— That's why I'm irritated. I could've had a different reaction, I could've used all calm and balanced words that I would find, and, in the end, I would listen to the same story: "You distort the facts, you're not humble, you won't admit that you're wrong". These are the arguments by not accepting the submissive positions people tried to impose. If Davi wants to know people's opinions, he can ask each one, I don't care, on the contrary.

— Davi has an immense love for his father. He hasn't overcome your separation.

— ...His father and him on this absurd idea... Two votes against one. I lost.

My advice, which was already difficult to assimilate, turned to mud, my own presence irritated him, and John's too. When he worked the night shift, I'd give him a ride to the restaurant and then go to the hospital. He came into my room to see if I was ready, the door was slightly open.

— I'm almost ready Davi! — I said while putting some lipstick on. I saw through the mirror him looking at the double bed and leaving angry.

Before getting in the car, his jacket fell on the floor, he kicked it, which landed in a puddle.

— Don't do that, Davi! — he took it and threw it on the back seat.

— I'm going to leave this house!

He put on a CD and stayed quiet until the restaurant. I didn't say anything. "When anger overpowers, it's best not to give it strength." I reminded myself of this thought. Sometimes I could do it.

I called John, as soon as I arrived at the hospital:

— Davi is so out of himself… he said he is leaving.

— I saw the scene from the office window, I think it's great for him to take this decision. It's time to grow up! My children don't live with me anymore, look at Harry, his age, working, paying rent. Don't you think it's time for Davi to do the same?

That same night, Davi asked to be transferred to a restaurant in London. We were in January of 2014. The house was already sad and empty, like me. Was not enough take out_the spider webs and hanging paintings. The cracks were still on the wall and grew when bothered.

One afternoon when I entered the kitchen, I saw him sitting down on the dinner table, next to the fireplace, with his laptop listening to music and typing. He had a calm expression on his face.

— Davi, I had a weird dream with you.

— Is it? — looked at me curiously and quickly without stopping to type.

— Davi, stop smoking this crap!

— What's up, Mrs. Flávia? I'm chill…

— Davi, I mean it! Please!

— Don't worry about me, I know about myself! — he said while putting his headphones and moving his head at the song rhythm.

It wasn't often that I saw him around the house, only when John was away, traveling. He hardly went to the gym anymore. There was a big lawn in the neighborhood, where football games always took place on weekends, but he showed no interest anymore. "Where was that passion?" — I asked myself.

I once met one of Davi's colleagues from the restaurant downtown and arranged to have a meeting so they could get to know our house. After a few days, I posted messages on Facebook to remind her the gathering and asked how Davi was at work.

— He is fine, but I have noticed he has gotten quieter since Joyce, Bel, and Israel left. It's a difficult phase, but it's going to go by.

— Yes, there were a lot of changes these past months. It would be great if you could come to a party, cheer him up.

— Alright, I'll talk to the guys.

— Oh… Please, don't let him know that we talked, he doesn't like it when I intrude on his life…

— Don't worry!

When she approached Davi to arrange the party, he soon realized I was behind it. He came home furious, asking if I had said anything about him to someone at the restaurant. I tried to cover it up.

— I bumped into Luana downtown, but it's been a month.

— What did you say about me?

— Nothing much, I asked if you were okay and invited her husband, her and the guys from the restaurant over. Is there a problem with that?

— You're ruining my life! You didn't have to say anything to anyone.

— Hey! I haven't said anything about you! I only asked how you were, which is suuuuuper normal, any mom on the planet does that.

— She is treating me differently; you must have said something. I am moving to a different restaurant, you're destroying me!

— Would stop this nonsense. No one is destroying you. It's okay. Stop that, Davi!

He went to his room, and I ran to my laptop and deleted all the messages I exchanged with Luana. After a while, he called me into his room and asked me to show him my conversations on Facebook with her.

69

— Stop this paranoia, I won't do that!

— If you don't have anything to hide, then show me!

— I won't! Any conversation with anyone by text is private, I don't have to show you anything!

— You don't want to show because you're talking about me to people! That's what you're hiding!

— Fine Davi, just for you to stop once and for all with nonsense, OK?

I opened my Facebook page and clicked on my messages with Luana. They were all there! I don't know why maybe I had clicked the wrong button; I just know they were all there.

— You haven't talked to anyone, right? Here is the proof of your lie, ruining your son's life.

— Davi, what is written that is ruining my son's life? Are you crazy?

— Now, everyone will look at me differently, treat me differently, and it's your fault!

— You are kidding, right? Do you think that because-I-invited-your-friend-with-whom-you're-working-with-and-some-of-your-friends-to-our-house is going to make them treat you differently?

He was still nervous, wasn't listening. So, I said to get his attention:

— Ok, Davi. Do you believe I'm destroying your life? I'm going to write on Facebook: "Mom destroys her son's life because she asks his friend how he is doing at work."

He stared at my seriously and said:

— Fine, just don't talk to anyone else. No one! — stressed aloud.

There was something wrong with Davi's mind. That wasn't just a rebellion of its age. It wasn't!

During that week, I heard tense conversations between his girlfriend and him over the phone.

— You haven't visited your girlfriend in a while, are you guys okay?

— No, we aren't.

— What happened?

— I've been cheated on — he answered full of bitterness.

— Ah… That's why it wasn't supposed to work… — I tried quickly to find some words that could help him come out of that stage, see the situation from a different angle — When it isn't supposed to be, it's best that it ends fast so that you can find the right person.

— I've been cheated on! Do you know what that means? Do you how I'm feeling?

— It isn't easy, I know, but don't keep brooding this pain… Only think that she doesn't deserve you and move on!

I hid in the living room to close my eyes and sigh. How can I protect myself from storms if the roof is full of gaps, and the skin, full of infiltrations? Love calms down, love protects, love recognizes, love accepts, love overcomes. Without love, it is easier to get lost in the pitfalls of disconnected, vague, unreal thoughts…

I was missing playful, restless, chatting, Davi. Those last two months were too long and heavy. I kept waiting for a good time when I could start a conversation.

— Davi, did you know therapy is something very good?

— Why don't you do it then? Don't come to me with that.

— I even started about three times, but I couldn't afford it. This one is online, isn't interesting? You don't need to leave home, and they're Brazilians… It's much better to talk in our language, don't you think?

I knew it wouldn't be easy to persuade him. He often heard people he admired, discrediting therapies and therapists, for lack of knowledge, saying, "Whoever has a friend doesn't need a therapist." I had already done research on that clinic; I was just trying to be natural. The director herself told me that the best way for those who oppose treatment is to do a session without compromise. Most people like it and want to keep going.

— I have already told you not to start on that subject matter!

I raised my tone and put strength in my words. Sometimes, yes, they find a way:

— Davi, you have nothing to lose! It's good to talk, unlock the things that are on the way, undo the knots. If it doesn't help, it won't get in the way of anything. You choose the person by her profile, look — I said showing the webpage on the laptop. — You can choose it by beauty too — I joked. — You only have to check the availability and schedule the time that you want.

— I won't talk to women. Women are full of fuss and don't know anything.

— The sessions are already paid for. If don't like it, don't need to continue.

He never accessed the page of the online clinic. A while later, I insisted:

— Davi, why don't you talk to Paul?

— What Paul?

— John's friend, that comes here once awhile. He is so nice, don't you think? He is a counselor!

— What's that?

— His job is to help people to overcome their problems by listening, counseling, and talking.

Useless, he wouldn't accept anything that had something to do with John. Davi was closing in on himself, isolating himself, becoming increasingly impenetrable. Without letting him know, I tried sharing my anguish, seek advice, opinions, a light that would pull him out of that hole.

— Don't worry, Flávia, it'll pass. He's confused, he still doesn't know how to deal with his feelings, he's full of doubts, he needs to revolve around this past, he's reorganizing his thoughts, it's just a phase. My nephew went through something like that, moved out, spent a year banging his head here and there, and came back a completely different person. This is all learning; you will see how good it will be for Davi this experience in London.

"Yes, yes, yes, everything it's going to be alright", I repeated to myself trying to undo that bitter taste of the days.

Chapter 7

The position in the restaurant in London turned up, and Davi needed to find a place to live quickly. He asked me for help. I realized his fragility in the face of the pressure in which all that change involved. I called some contacts and got him a room to share with another boy. The person in charge of the flat was a Brazilian, who didn't demand a deposit and left Davi at ease to stay as long as he wanted, if he did not like it or if it was unfit for work, he would be free to move.

London doesn't fit itself. London has many faces and speaks many languages. If it's easy losing yourself, it's not hard to find it. There Davi went looking for the challenges he needed to live, without knowing the size of those he already had in him.

Even though he was far from the restaurant and had to face long waiting for buses in the freezing dawns of February, as there was no sub-way late at night, Davi did not want to look for another place to live. The friend who gave me the indication said that the Brazilian was a very nice person, which explained his decision to stay. We communicated only what was necessary. He wanted distance, and I tried to respect that time. He had disappeared from Facebook too, rarely posted anything or even disabled his page for days. He once posted a picture of a forearm with a big tattoo, a Chinese word. "Is that you, Davi?" — I sent a message from my cell phone. No answer. On the photo, the person was wearing a striped shirt I didn't know. Coincidentally, John was in the dining room talking to a Chinese client on Skype. I asked for permission and showed him the tattoo.

— Can you tell me what that word means?

— It means "respect."

𝄢

About thirty days after he moved, Davi asked me to bring a suitcase with clothes he had left behind. I wanted so much to see him, to know how he was, to know his new home, to go out, to talk. We set the day. He waited for me at the station in London. I walked along the platform, towards the roulette wheel that gave access to the exit, when I saw, under the jacket he was wearing, the striped shirt, the same as the Facebook photo. I said smiling with the discovery:

— It's you, Davi!!! The tattoo...

He rehearsed a little smile, picked up his bag and we walked to the flat. I saw he'd lost a lot of weight.

— Don't you eat at the restaurant you work at?

— Sometimes.

The neighborhood was beautiful and pleasant. Near the station, there was a good business area just about four blocks from where he lived. The flat was simple, organized and clean. He shared a room with an English boy. There was no one home. We left the suitcase and went out to eat. He was very quiet. I tried to talk animatedly to keep a good energy between us. We went to an Italian restaurant. He ordered Bolognese spaghetti, and I ordered a calzone. He couldn't eat, had two bites, said he wasn't hungry. My calzone was delicious, but I ate only one piece, I said I wasn't hungry either, and asked the waiter to wrap it. I'd leave it for him to eat later. I'm sure he was eating very badly. I had looked at the refrigerator almost empty. In the cupboard, just a couple of packets of instant noodles and a box of cereal.

— I know what you're going through, I've had depression. You lose your hunger; your voice gets stuck... You need to see a doctor.

While I was talking, he was rubbing his hands nervously. He got up and went to the sidewalk. Walking back to the flat, we passed in front of a supermarket.

— That supermarket is very expensive. Isn't there another one in the area? — I asked.

— No.

— Is this where you shop?

— Sometimes.

— Shall we go inside? I want to buy some things for you.

I was surprised when he put in the basket a ready-made salad tray that cost five pounds, he didn't look at the price.

— When you're doing your shopping, look for offers and look for the expiration date, otherwise your money will go away without you seeing it!

But apparently, he wasn't spending it on food at all. I left the groceries at the flat, and since he wasn't comfortable with me, I said goodbye.

— Spend a day off in Brighton, we can drive around, go to many places... Oh, don't forget the calzone, I left it on the microwave, it's delicious!

I left very worried. I got home and e-mailed his dad that I didn't like what I saw and that Davi definitely needed to go to the doctor. Shortly after, I received messages from Davi: "What did you tell dad? Stop destroying my life, stop spreading the word that I'm sick, you just ruin me!", he ended up swearing and disappeared again from Facebook.

A few days later, I received a phone call from Angelina, Bel's mom, Israel's ex-girlfriend. We go very acquainted when our children started dating. Bel was living in Rio de Janeiro, but Davi and her kept their friendship, never lost touch, unless on the times he would disappear. On one of these conversations, Davi mentioned he was thinking of killing himself. Bel took at a joke, asked him to stop with that nonsense, but she got scared and told her mom about it, and she called me. I felt a chill ruining through my body, I was speechless. Angelina tried not to make me worried:

— These kids say all kinds of things... Look, nothing will happen, because whoever wants to commit suicide, don't send messages, right?

— Thank you, Angelina, for letting me know...

I went to the computer warned his dad about it.

— Go pick him up right now — he ordered me.

— He hates me, if I go, I believe it will be worse.

I didn't want to ask for John's help, it wouldn't be a good idea involving him in it. I got Fred and went to the park nearby, so I could phone someone without John listening to it. I was confused, thinking of s lot of things at the same time. I had to be calm... Who could help? Who? Someone who Davi trusted without realizing I was interfering. Difficult. "The Brazilian guy", I thought, "responsible for the flat... He doesn't know me, and my friend he is a very nice guy. But how am I going to talk to him? I'm going to have to say it, come clean, there's no other way."

— Hello Ricardo, I'm Davi's mom. I really need to talk to you, but Davi can't know about it.

— You can say it!

— I'm going through a very delicate situation, I need your help. Davi isn't emotionally well, he is depressed and said to a friend that he is thinking about killing himself. I have no one to ask for help, because he won't talk about these issues with anyone. I realized that he has great admiration for you...

That was the way! I was relieved. I felt that this boy was a suitable person to talk to Davi. He told me he arrived in London at the age of eighteen and had been living there for ten years. He said he'd had some difficult experiences in life and told me of some cases. I could feel in his voice that he was an honest guy with a good heart.

— Don't worry, rest assured, I'll talk to him. I won't let him know you called me. I'll get that idea out of his head, and you can call me anytime, no problem. As soon as I talk to him, I'll give you a call back.

I went to the hospital, but I couldn't work. My heart ached, endless anguish. I didn't know if I should call him for news, if I should wait for him to call me. It might be too late... I couldn't just stand there. I went to my boss's office in the other building. He was alone. He was new to the company. He didn't know me. I asked him to talk and I explained, crying, what was happening.

— How old is your son? — he asked.

— Eighteen.

— He's of legal age, there's nothing you can do, there's nothing anyone can do.

He wrote down his cell phone number on a piece of paper and gave it to me:

— If you need anything, you can call me. Now, get back to work, you better keep your mind on the job.

I picked up the paper with the phone and left thinking: "What help can he give me if he just told me there is nothing to do? I have to do something, even if it is going to London now and begging Davi not to end his life! I won't just stand here!" I threw my uniform in the slot, grabbed my purse and went home. I had messages and missed calls from Joyce. No calls from Ricardo. I walked right by John in the hall.

— You're early, did something happen?

— Davi told Bel that he is thinking about killing himself.

— ...there's nothing you can do about it.

I lost my mind and started screaming:

— You English, what are you? An ice rock? "There's nothing you can do! There's nothing you can do!" Is that all you can say? There has to be! There has to be! I'll do something, anything! Anything but stand here and wait for the worst to happen!

I left the house. I went for a walk to think. I was in no condition to drive to London. Would I take a train? And getting there, what would happen? Would Davi receive me? Would he be aggressive with me? What if the boy was talking to him and I blew it? No, I can't go like this. Better wait for the phone call...

Five minutes later, I sent Ricardo a message:

— Any news?

— Davi's working now, when he gets here, I'll talk. Rest assured.

Joyce called me:

— Mom, have you heard from Davi? Bel told me. He's not answering his cell phone or answering his messages, he's off Facebook...

— I asked for help from the Brazilian who lives with him in the flat, I think he is the best person to talk to Davi. He will call me later. Stay calm, daughter, everything will be fine.

77

I couldn't sleep. I looked at my cell phone, I rolled in bed, I walked around the house. I spent the whole night with that anguish. In the morning, I sent a message to Ricardo. He didn't answer. Around eleven o'clock, he called me.

— I saw your message, but I was late, now we can talk calmly. I waited for Davi to arrive from the restaurant, I like him a lot, he's very focused. I talked to him, subtly, without letting him know that I was onto something. I told my story, because my life wasn't easy! I told him my hard times, everything I've been through with dad, with mom, but we have to move on, we have to stand firm. I said that everything bad could happen in my life, but that I would never end it, because there is always a way for everything. A lot of faith in God! It was a good talk, it was positive, I think he's fine, he'll come out of this.

— Ricardo, I can't thank you enough, you were an angel, truly an angel that appeared in his life!

— No worries, I'm here for that! God blesses.

I was so afraid to ask for help, from the boy's reaction, who doesn't even know me. He could blame me for compromising him, for putting this "bomb" in his hands, but no, he did not make any judgment. He offered himself with an open heart. He lost a few hours of sleep, waited for Davi to arrive at dawn, and I am sure that conversation was very, very important at that moment.

Sometimes, I'd pass messages trying to be very natural: "Hey, Davi, what's up?", "Working hard?", "Are you enjoying the academy?" — he wouldn't answer. When he got in touch with Joyce, Bel or his Father they'd let me and each other know. A news network was formed to alleviate the anguish of endless periods of silence. I needed to know more: how he was in the house, if he was sad, quiet, eating, going out, talking, having fun.... So, I'd call Ricardo. "It's okay," he'd answer without giving details. Ricardo didn't know Davi from before, he had no parameters to evaluate. I looked like an overprotective mom, who bothered.

— Can you meet me at Brighton station tonight at 7 p.m.?

I got scared when I saw Davi's message on my cell phone.

— Yes, I can. Wait for me in the parking lot.

I called the hospital and told them I wouldn't be at work that night. I didn't notice any positive changes. He was still thin, only saying the necessary.

— Shall we go to the marina and get something to eat? — I asked.

— Let's go.

— How's the restaurant?

His face changed.

— They're transferring me to another neighborhood — he said upset, — right now that the manager was becoming my friend. The other day I stayed until 2 a.m. helping him solve a problem.

— Wow, and how did you get home?

— By bus I waited two hours for the bus.

— Yeah... Transportation at night is complicated... And the gym?

— There's no time, just on the days off.

— And how's the house?

He grimaced.

— But didn't you say the guy, the Brazilian, was good people?

— Yeah, but I forgot dope on the stove, he got mad at me.

— And the Latino?

— I don't even see him.

— What about the Englishman who shares the room with you?

— We barely talk.

— Ah...

— What did the people in Brazil say about me having gone to London?

— Ah... They thought it was great, right, Davi? London is London!

— Is that all?

— I haven't been in touch much, you asked me not to talk about you...

— Do you have the phone number of the Brazilian where I live, Ricardo?

— No, I don't.

We had been walking around the marina looking for a restaurant.

— Shall we go to this one? — he suggested it.

— Let's go!

He ordered a bottle of mineral water. He couldn't choose, he didn't know the dishes, he looked with no patience to the menu.

— How about noodle? You really like noodles!

— That's okay.

I ordered and went to the bathroom so. I could erase Ricardo's number of my phone.

He was noticeably quiet. When the meal arrived, he started eating slowly. All the sudden he started weeping tears, tears that he held back and could not control. He wiped his face with a napkin and said:

— Get the check.

It was not a good place to talk. I paid the check and we left.

— Davi, you cannot stay like this, Davi… Please…

— Take me to the station.

— I will, but we will talk, you came here for this.

— We'll talk when we get there.

We headed silently. Thinking about how I could approach the subject. Words to break down that barrier needed to be found. I stopped the car on the parking lot. I had to be quick and firm.

— Davi, face the situation head on, as strong and firm as you are! You need treatment! What is wrong with that? Thousands of people go through the same problem: artists, famous people, people you see from the outside and think "Wow, this person is great" — but they are not! They are full of problems, hurt inside. And what do they do? They seek for help, go to the doctor, get treatment, and everything will be fine again!

He was tense, swallowing those words that rolled like stones down his throat, frozen hands. He opened the door as soon as I finished that short speech and walked to the station.

I called the guy again I, wanted to ask him to convince Davi to get a treatment, but this time I realized that he did not seem to have the necessary patience to deal with this situation.

— Yeah, I told Davi to focus on work, but, on the contrary, he asked for two weeks of vacation and now it is worse. It complicates it.

It is never, never easy to take care of someone with depression. You must love them very much and be close at all times. It can take time, and each one has its own life to take care of, its own problems. Besides, people don't know how to help. They don't understand the disease, they often think it is whininess or quite simple to seek treatment. I suffered thinking about the weight Davi was carrying all by himself. How difficult it was to work, to focus, and people insisting on this path that, in fact, only worsens, because a depressive person feels under enormous tension when performing any task, how simple it may be, and every mistake or badly put comment about it, pushes it deeper and deeper into themselves. The thoughts are disorganized causing despair, and the person not understanding what it is going on, trying to hold on a smile while working and, inside, a bomb is about to explode. That is what I felt.

What idea was rooted in his mind that wouldn't let him seek for help? Why couldn't he tell anyone? Why did he believe that he was destroyed? What would be the misconceptions that many ignorant people insist on propagating and that he learned so well, solidified within him? Would it be that "depression is a woman's thing"; or "depression is a weakness"; or "it is because he doesn't have a work to do"; or all of it together and more? If people understood how destructive it can be, what they only consider a "simple statement" when it comes to a affected mind, they would certainly not want to be responsible for such a cruelty, and on the opposite, they would try to help. Why did he demand himself so much? Why? His father was the right person to help him, for the love, the connection between them, the admiration that Davi felt for him. He was the person that he listened and respected the most. However, whenever his dad talked about it Davi would disappear, causing my agony to multiply a thousand times. I was living terrified. I would get scared when my phone rang, when I received a message, when I opened my computer. I would pray, pray, and pray asking him to have positive thoughts and accept treatment.

𝄢

Joyce and some friends were taking a trip to some European countries and would spend a few days in London and Brighton. Davi and her messaged each other to set up meetings, tours. That is good news! Anything that took him out of his nebulous reality would be very welcomed. When Joyce arrived in London, in April, the day was beautiful, sunny. They met in Hyde Park, drank beer together and took some pictures, which Joyce posted on Facebook. He was still skinny, thin hair, had no expression of joy, a weak, forced smile. Even though he had a strong bond with his sister, he would also get angry and disappear whenever she talked about a doctor, about treatment.

A few days later, Davi messaged me saying that he had quit the restaurant and that was going to Brazil for two weeks. I called him:

— Did something happen?

— I will tell you later. I found a ticket on the internet for eight hundred pounds. I am going to buy it.

— Did you research well? I can try to find one with a better price.

I was going to buy the ticket. I thought it was great, because then I could control the return date. I did not want him to stay only two weeks in Brazil. I wanted him to have enough time to go to an appointment, start a treatment and even stay there. Gently, his dad would be able to take him to the doctor and everything would be settled. In that moment I had high hopes. I got a cheaper ticket, with a return date for two months. He did not like it, stated that he needed to be back in two weeks, that he had plans, but I did not care about the complaints. That time was needed.

— Don't worry Davi, everything will be fine, you will find a better job, maybe somewhere else, living in London is expensive and tough, don't you think? You got to catch a subway, stay up late at a bus stop… Patience, everything will work out! Go to Brazil, chill out, enjoy!

Upset, he asked me:

— Can you bring me that grey suitcase? The one I have here is too big.

—Yes, I can.

— Can you take the big suitcase to Brighton with my things? I am leaving the rented room, getting out of the house.

— Please?

— Yeah... Please...

— I sure can, no problem.

We agreed that I would take the suitcase on the eve of his trip, so he had time to pack his luggage. Before I left home, I received a message:

— Do you still have those pictures from when we were kids? — he asked referring to his siblings.

— Of course, I do!

— Can you bring them to me?

— Fine, I will.

At the small building's gate, I messaged that I had arrived. He did not answer. I called; he did not answer. I waited a little longer, nothing. I called again, no life signal. I felt my body weak and trembling. Bad thoughts mingled with loose phrases, memories of conversations, and tears rolled confusedly on my face: "I've been through much worse things and I've never had depression," "He needs a girlfriend," "He needs to work," "With all he's got, he still has depression?", "If he dies, we bury him." A noise behind me scared me and made me turn suddenly. It was him slamming the door, carrying a suitcase and a bag. I wiped my face disguising it.

— Davi, your flight is tomorrow! Why are you carrying these bags?

— I won't stay here anymore. Do you have a pen?

— What is happening? – I thought that they had lost patience with him and had an argument. It was better to leave then. I handed the pen.

— Have you brought my football shirt that I asked?

— I did, it is here! – I answered getting it out of the bag.

— This one is a gift for "the guy", now this pen is so I can write a message for that douche.

— Davi, don't get into trouble, you are already leaving anyways.

— Leaving with my head up, just as I came in — he said while walking up the stairs.

— Is someone there, Davi? – I yelled.

— No.

We left by the street, me pulling one of the suitcases, him another one and carrying a big sports bag, with the strap crossed over his chest. His face rigid, his walk heavy.

— Did you bring the pictures?

I got an envelope out of my bag and handed to him. He stopped walking, opened the envelope and stood there looking, one by one.

— In here I was happy. These were the best moments of my life – he said filled with sadness.

— Davi, that is in the past… Don't get attached to it!

— I was happy there, with my brother, my dad, my friends, playing soccer at the square. Look at what you have done with me! — yelled at with his eyes full of tears, with rancor, hurt.

— Davi, that was your childhood, we are on different times. Don't think like this… I did what I thought was best.

The pictures fell on the ground. Some on the sidewalk, the others on the street. We crouched down to get it. People passed by dodging. Two picked up a few and handed to us. We walked in silent to the station.

— Do you have somewhere to go, a friend you can stay at until tomorrow?

— No.

— Shall we look for a hotel close to the airport?

— Are you going to stay with me?

— Yeah, I will stay with you till tomorrow, I will take you to the airport. Be patient, everything will be fine.

We were waiting at the platform for a train to the Victoria Station and, from there, we would head to the airport.

— You ruined my life, my dreams, my plans, everything! — said out loud.

Few others that were there heard and moved away.

— Davi, you have not even started to live yet!

— Look at me, look at what I am!

— You are only eighteen! All your life is still ahead of you!

Trains passing by at full speed made me extremely anxious, we needed to leave that place urgently. When I looked at the billboard, I saw that our train was next. There were a lot of free seats. We sat side-by-side. I got out of my bag a small can full of Rescue candy.

— Want one?

He accepted it. Then asked for another one. I handed him the entire can:

— You can have them

He read the label.

— This is a medicine, isn't it?

— It is a floral. It helps maintain our temper.

By his facial expression, I knew that he wouldn't use it. Either way, I put it in his backpack.

A voice message warned that a system problem was forcing all passengers to get off at the next station. The train platform was full, the billboards had no sign of when services would resume. I ended up getting a cab.

— Where are you guys headed? — asked the driver.

— To the Victoria Station. From there, we will catch a train to the Gatwick airport — I answered.

— How much do you charge to get us to the Gatwick? – asked Davi.

— It is expensive! – I said quickly, giving the driver no time to answer.

— Why can't you let the driver and I come to a deal? – he asked angry.

— They negotiate, we just need to chat. You prune me, you don't allow me to be myself. See how you treat me? See how you raised me?

— Stop it, Davi, stop! I just made a comment! If we don't save ten here, five there, money disappears. There is no need for that, the train is faster and cheaper — I said with low voice, firmly looking him in his eyes. He kept talking, blaming me. I turned my face to the window, looking down the street, crying, thinking, "What do I do?"

I wondered if I had better get out of the cab and leave, but I turned to him and said,

— It is a lot of love, Davi... A lot of love.

Love and understanding for something I did not know what it was. Something that was going on in his mind. In rebellion, the person is herself, even if very wounded, even if she comes out of herself, that she is domi-nated by anger, even if her anguish, her conflicts, she doesn't lose herself as I saw how Davi did. There was another intensity in the look, words, expressions, and only those who know him as well as I do could see it. He was suffering immensely, and I wouldn't leave him all alone. "If accusing me is needed for him to clean his basements, to free those ghosts that are tormenting him, I'll let him do it, just so I can help him". I thought.

He wanted to get into the first hotel we saw, without even asking the price. I asked him to have a juice or a coffee while we searched the Internet for a better offer. We got a great room near the airport. The flight to Brazil was the next day, at eight in the evening. We would still spend several hours together. I texted John, said I was in trouble, did not get into any details, would explain everything when I get back.

The next day Davi woke up feeling better, airy, had a chill counte-nance. He organized his suitcase, separating everything he did not want, to be donated later. We left the luggage at the hotel and took a bus to the nearest town. We went to the mall, where we had a snack. Later we went to some stores, he bought himself a shirt with the England flag on it and two gifts, one for Bia, and the other to her mom, always asking what I thought about it. We walked around when I realized he got tense. His face, hands, breathing, lack of patience. I thought he was about to blame me, repeat those emotions and curse.

— Where is the drug store? Can you help me find one? – I asked anxious.

— What happened? Are you ok?

— A horrible toothache. Wow... I need medicine urgently.

We headed to the drug store, I bought the medicine I needed, asked for a cup of water and pretended to take it in.

He got worried, and every now and then I complained about the pain again. It seemed as it worked because he did not have any attacks. On the bus, while we were returning to the hotel to pick up our bags, he began talking to a young Chilean couple, new to England, seated next to the door. He gave them tips, told some stories, made jokes about it... That was the real Davi: talkative, helpful, interested, friendly, cheerful. This situation would go by and he would return to be the same Davi from before.

I said goodbye to him at the airport asking him not to forget to charge his phone so we could stay in touch during his stopover in Madrid.

I got home around 9 p.m. I was exhausted, feeling down. I put my purse down on the couch so I could stroke Fred. I heard a noise in the kitchen. It was John, who asked me if everything was okay with Davi. I did not answer. I felt my body stiffen and tears flow. He approached surprised and hugged me:

— What happened, sweetheart?

I could not speak.

— What is happening?

— Davi is not well.

I stood there, laid on the couch, John tried to calm me down saying that I was not alone.

— Anyone who is not okay goes to the doctor. Why does he refuse? That is stupid! – he said.

— John, it seems that Davi doesn't figure that out, he cannot see it this way.

John could not understand either, he could not see. I knew that look with no answers and the frown on his forehead.

Chapter 8

I woke up with the memory of a bad dream with Davi, he was inside a wheel, the water spinning, his head out of the whirlwind. In my intuition there was marijuana involved. I opened the computer to research the symptoms I observed in Davi. I found a medical website in the United States related to the use of narcotics that answered questions online. I reported the facts, the symptoms, his behavioral changes, told them that he was not an addict, that he smoked from time to time, and asked if the condition was reversible. The website's doctor reported back generically, of course, each case is different and needs to be analyzed properly before a final diagnosis, but confirmed that there are histories of paranoia, aggressiveness and other disorders caused by marijuana use, even for a short period and not only in dependents, and that the tendency of these symptoms was to gradually disappear as soon as the person stopped using it. That was the answer I needed, at least at that moment. I don't know what happened when he was in London, if he used any drugs, but it was likely that he was so upset in those days because of it. It made sense.

I talked to Joyce, Israel, and texted his father. We had to raise Davi's awareness of the marijuana-induced disorders in the brain of some users that were not disclosed, barely known. We had to show him the harm it was doing to his life. Most users ignore the harmful effects of marijuana, seeing them only as arguments from an oppressive society that wants to marginalize them. Davi would know how to discern.

I looked at the clock. Davi was still on the plane, heading to São Paulo. There, he would stay two days at Bia's parents' house before going to Belo Horizonte. I messaged her:

— Bia, darling, what is up? Can you send word about Davi, please? But don't let him know, he is very independent, doesn't like me asking. Moms are moms! I am a momma bear!

— Leave it to me, Flávia, I will let you know.

She messaged me sometimes, always saying everything was fine. In Belo Horizonte, Davi went out with his friends, cousins, father, brothers. I followed him from afar. My mom knew he was depressed and wouldn't admit undergoing any kind of treatment. After a long conversation the two had in the kitchen, Davi, filling her with questions about her past, wondering how her childhood was, her father, her mom, her siblings, and their relationships, she felt comfortable gifting him a book about depression. That word had the power to enter his mind and devastate the solid image he had of himself and that he needed at all costs to maintain. It was something beyond his ability to understand. Angry, he left home and disappeared for a few days. Some of his friends were also in the "marijuana phase", which obviously made our path even more difficult. He was "blocked," did not care about silly advices.

One night, Israel, Joyce and her boyfriend called Davi to eat a hamburger near home. They were all happy, eating, drinking, talking. Joyce had gone to the bathroom and, when she returned, saw Davi breaking a beer bottle on Israel's head, and her boyfriend, holding him. The reason was a comment from Israel, who wanted to take advantage of that moment of relaxation to send his message to his brother:

— Dude, stop using drugs!

When I heard about it, I remembered an accusation Davi made when we were in London in the taxi: "You didn't let me be a normal child, you didn't let me fight with my brother like every child does." I tried to find a reason for him to say that. The two had sibling fights even as teenagers. Why didn't he remember that? Where would he have gotten that idea and why was it stronger than reality? I looked for references from a good male psychiatrist, since he did not want to talk to a woman, and I passed on the contact to his father.

— Try to convince him because he only listens to you.

He couldn't do it.

The day of his returning trip was coming when I received a new message:

— Mom, I don't know what to do. I don't know if I am staying here or coming back.

— You were not happy here, Davi. Stay with your brothers, with your father.

Coming back without treatment was not a good option. If his father, who he loved so much, could not convince him, it would be impossible with me.

— I have no home here.

— What about that plan of you guys living together, you, Israel, and your father? Did you guys talk about it? I can pay the rent and you split the expenses. Who knows Beto doesn't cheer up either?

Beto was the older brother of his father's other relationship. They got along well, it would be a good opportunity for coexistence, experiences, and a new perspective of life could emerge from it. As he had free time, Davi oversaw the search for the apartment, so he would get more involved in the process of moving in, talking, pointing out, interacting, being helpful. That is what I imagined, but it was not an easy task because of the depression that kept taking over. Just so I could try to help, I picked up some ads on the internet and passed on to him. It did not work either.

— Hi, Davi, did you find any interesting apartments today?

— No. I cannot see myself here.

— But that is a matter of time, you will adapt again, you will see.

— I cannot get a job.

— That too is a matter of time. You just need to do the treatment, and everything will...

No one knew for sure where he was going and what he was doing. I was afraid of losing him forever. They were all busy during the day working. He was alone, wandering, unable to find himself, unable to resolve his conflicts, sinking into them even more. He once told his father that he spent hours of the early morning talking to a homeless man downtown.

It would have been three months since he was in Brazil.

— Mom, I need to talk to you.

I saw the message and called immediately.

— Hey, Davi, is everything all right?

— Mom, can you help me get back?

— Davi, you were not well here...

— I know, but it will be different now. I have given it a lot of thought; I want to go back and study. I cannot handle staying here. When I start working, I will pay you for the ticket.

— What about the apartment plan with your father and brothers?

— I don't see myself here, I cannot, I don't feel well, I tried, there is no point. I want to study, I want to go to College, will you help me?

— You tried that, remember?

— But now it is going to be different, I was very lost, now I want to study, I don't want to stay here.

— If you don't get a treatment, no place is going to be good for you, Davi, none!

— If you stop saying I am crazy, depressed, it already helps a lot.

— Davi...

— Will you help me?

— Let us think about it calmly. Let us talk, OK?

I felt he was even more lost than before, inside and out. No links, no connection, no place. He could not identify with Brazil or England. He was rootless. I tried to analyze, understand, comprehend; tried to find a way to help him. His dad, two brothers and Joyce worked all day. I had time for him, had left my job at the hospital, was working from home. Wherever he stayed, he would need a motivation to start over. It came from him the desire to study. This was a sparkling ray of light, signaling thought in the future. He was saying he wouldn't give in to marijuana, he was reasoning, discerning, was not dominated by it, as I came to think. If I said "no" at that moment, I could put everything to waste, cause a frustration capable of immediately throwing it in "its" arms, and I was too afraid that "it" would never let him go again. Leo was gone from England. Davi knew that he could count on me, that I was his home, his family. I saw a single hope I could not lose. I needed to keep him balanced until all that was over. Every attitude, every decision was a risk.

At the big house, we were receiving young students of different nationalities, which would be very good for Davi to divert his focus from John, from his problems, and perhaps, in a new friendship, in conversation, a voice could penetrate that darkness. It was early July. Classes would start in September, but he needed to be there to enroll. I prepared John for Davi's return. He was apprehensive, however, seeing as how I became the very expectation of saving my son, he didn't want to be the hindrance. A few days before the trip, Joyce told me that she talked to Davi.

— Mom, he told me he is coming back because he needs to help you, he said he wants to separate you from John.

I looked at the clock. It was only a few hours before he boarded when I got his message on the cellphone:

— I need to talk, call me.

— Hey, son, is everything ready for the trip?

— Yeah, but I wanted to tell you that I am not going to Brighton. I am going to Coventry.

— Oh... So, you have changed your mind? Why?

— I don't want to stay there with John.

— Davi, you must put your goals in your head and move on! You told me you want to study, didn't you? So, forget about John, live your life, go to College and that is it. Here you live for free, you have my help, everything is much easier!

— No, I cannot. I already made up my mind.

— Ok then, go to Coventry. I think it is going to be good for you.

— Will you come with me?

— What do you mean?

— Live there with me.

— Live? Oh, no way! My life is here, my work is here. I just got out of the hospital after six years cleaning it, I am working from home, I cannot give up what I have and start all over again. My life is quiet now.

— No way then? — I felt his voice suppressed.

— No, I cannot.

— Is this your final word? — he seemed to cry.

— Yes, have a nice flight. We talk later.

I walked around the room with my hands on my head. What do I do, oh Lord? What do I do? Among some objects on the dresser, I saw a picture of them when they were kids, happy, framed in the past, sickening my heart. I filled myself with guilt. I remembered the story I read on the Internet about mental disorders in people who change countries. And now I was going to leave him all alone? What is the point of "all I've got" if I don't have anything? What is the point of being with someone if I cannot be with my sick son? It might have looked like I was playing his game, but I did not really care. I grabbed my phone and called him; he did not answer. Then I left a message: "I will go with you to Coventry. We meet tomorrow morning at the airport." After a while, I get his message, relieved: "Right on!"

I told John that Davi had changed his mind and was going to Coventry.

— Good, it is time to become independent, walk with his own legs.

I looked up John's agenda, he had a trip scheduled for the next day, which was good, because I did not want him seeing me leave, carrying a suitcase. I decided wouldn't say anything, he wouldn't understand. The next day, John woke up, turned on the TV and kept lying down, which I was surprised about.

— Do you travel today? – I asked

— No, I changed it, it is tomorrow.

— Ah...

— Davi arrives today, doesn't he?

— He does...

— You're not planning on picking him up at the airport, are you? He is big enough and already knows his way around.

I looked at him unresponsive and left the room. I took the bag in the basement and put it in the laundry room. I pretended I was doing laundry and packed my luggage any way I could. At noon I saw that John was asleep. The window of our room was facing the street, the curtain was closed. I kissed Fred and walked out the back door quietly.

I ran away from home

Chapter 9

Davi showed up at the arrival's hall wearing the t-shirt with the England's flag. It was a good sign. He smiled when he saw me and soon got serious again. I hugged him happily.

— Are we taking a train to Coventry? I asked

— Did you leave the car in Brighton?

— I sold it when I left the hospital. The was no need anymore. I used John's car whenever I had.

Once again, Angelina and Robson, Bel's mom and stepfather, welcomed us with a party: music, beer, delicious food and lively conversation. I went out to look for work all week long. Davi remade his resume and handed out to some restaurants. We went to the College, where he received various information about the courses available. He seemed fine but slept a lot. I needed help finding a place to live. I went to counsel at a government agency and explained the situation I was going through with my son.

— Unfortunately, there is nothing we can do. You reside in Brighton; you must look up for the government agency there.

I could not get back to Brighton and wait for the whole process. I tried talking to other people right there. The answer was always the same. A room to rent came up in a nearby town, in a Brazilian woman's house. Davi and I went there. The money I had would be enough to keep us for just a month. We had to get a job as soon as possible. I went out every day. Sometimes I was able to drag Davi with me.

On our second week, we went to the Labor Center to apply for the unemployment insurance, even against Davi's will. He definitely did not accept receiving any kind of government help, he had pride greater than needed.

— It is a temporary situation, Davi, once we are working, we won't be needing it anymore. There is no other way, the money is running out.

With the last few pounds, he had in the bank, he paid for a month on the gym, which was in the same neighborhood, which made me very happy. It was great to see him leave home to do a healthy activity. For the people who knew him, he was just a little sad, quiet.

One night, when I entered the room, he was leaning against the headboard of the bed with his laptop on his lap. I was folding some clothes, getting ready to sleep. Suddenly, I see him full of anger, revolted, his face tense, red and a cry stuck inside. He stared at the computer screen and held it tightly. Out of control, punched the screen.

— Davi! Don't do this!

It was already done. He stood there paralyzed while I was trying to understand the reason for that crisis. I took the laptop out of his hands, sat quietly by his side, and spent hours that night telling stories of people who have gone through terrible deprivations in their lives and who have been able to overcome, had the patience to wait for good opportunities, wisdom to face enemies and difficult times. He heard everything without saying a word, was getting calm until he fell asleep.

At the end of the month of July, the house owner's daughter went there to spend some time with her mom. Davi and her already knew each other from a party in Coventry. She was in College, in a nearby town, where she shared a flat with some colleagues. She had a boyfriend, was learning to drive, was going out with her friends, had a normal life. Sometimes Davi and her would talk in the kitchen; sometimes they would go to the gym together.

I ignored John's first messages. When he asked me when I was coming back, I would just say, "Take care of Fred, please." Later, I told him I wasn't coming back." Flávia, it is all here, the way you left it: me, your dog, your job and a place for Davi. If you don't come back, I'll come get you guys!" he insisted.

𝄢

I was walked around the yard one afternoon after the rain, when I saw in the sky a clear rainbow, a perfect semicircle right in front of the horizon. Davi was lying in his room. I went to the stairs and called him out.

— Davi, Davi! Come and look!

— What?

— Look how beautiful, Davi! I have never seen such a perfect rainbow like this one in my life!

He kept looking, trying to understand. Sometimes I felt Davi distant. He was not smoking pot, he was clean.

— And what does it mean? — I had not thought of any meanings, only about the beauty.

— Well... An ancient tale says that at the end of the rainbow, you can find a pot full of gold!

We sat there and talked for a while.

— Any news about the house? He asked.

— I am searching the neighborhoods nearby so that when we are able to rent, I'm at least aware of the region.

— What about that house you were told?

— No way. I had a bad feeling about the place, the house too...

— Brighton is a good city.

— It has a different energy, right? The name even says... Brighton... A sunny day in Brighton is so beautiful, the sea, the beach, the people, all those young students on the street...

— It is hard here...

— Yeah...

— What if we go back to Brighton? But you lost everything, didn't you? Your work, the house, John...

— John messaged me the other day. He said I still got my place there and you too, and if we need anything, we can count on him.

— Yeah... He really likes you. But I am not going back to that house. I want to take care of myself.

— It is different now, Davi, there are some students spending the season there, you don't have to worry about John, he is offering you a room, take the opportunity, Davi. As you can see, it is not easy for us to stay here... Focus on your studies, on your goals!

— Can you help me find a place? I don't want to stay here and live on the government's aid, it kills me.

— What about a doctor, therapy?

— I can take care of that. I cannot stand you on my head anymore. I need to stay away from you too.

If on the one hand I wanted to be with Davi, on the other I was taking away his chance to force himself into other relationships that could be useful, people who maybe, even without realizing it, could make him understand things differently, which I was not being able to.

I knew there was a room to rent at Cléber's house in Brighton. I had known him and his wife for few years now. He is a big guy, the kind of guy who demands respect, speaks firm, policeman type, passionate about cars and airplanes. The youngest son was living with them, a boy about Davi's age. They already knew each other from some football match. I felt a great possibility there. I called and told them to reserve the room for Davi.

Chapter 10

We found a hostel on the Internet in the center of Brighton, where he would stay temporarily. In the lobby, the atmosphere was relaxed, with many young people laughing and talking.

— Are you going to be okay here? – I asked

— All good.

John and Fred were waiting for me at home. He hugged me saying that he loved me and that everything was going to be okay. When the Italians arrived, we gathered in the room to celebrate my return. Two days later, I went to Cléber's house to take Davi and his luggage. Warm, talkative, he invited us for tea and told us how he ended up in Brighton. He said he got depressed in Brazil. Everything was walking backwards in his life.

— And how did you find treatment? — I asked.

— I cured myself by coming here. I am against treatment for depression. I got here, worked a lot, managed to stabilize myself and that is it! The depression was gone.

I knew those words entered Davi's mind and strengthened the idea that he did not need treatment. I felt weakened and without arguments listening to that story and remembering that my most difficult depression also vanished when I left Brazil. I still had no knowledge about all the levels of depression, and in Davi's case, there were still other problems that I wouldn't expose. However, he was more relaxed, and that family could be his inspiration, his impulse, a great environment to start his life over. I had faith that this would be the way.

When I sat down with John to continue my work, he said he had to make some changes and asked me to take care of some household expenses. I thought it was fair, I didn't care. When we moved in together, he wanted to spare me those worries so I could dedicate myself to my books, which I could not do it.

It was unbearably hot. When I went to put the recyclable residue in the boxes in front of the house, I saw Davi approaching. He was tired, sweaty. He sat on the sidewalk and asked for a bottle of water.

— Come in, Davi, let us get inside.

— No, I just want a bottle of water.

— There's no one home.

— Just water, please.

He took off his shoes and socks. He had some blisters on his feet.

— Did you come on foot?

— I did.

— Wow! Under this hot sun? Why didn't you take a bus?

— To save money.

— But it doesn't justify... We save money when buying clothes, for example: instead of buying fifty-pound pants, you buy a twenty, but on a hot day like this, walk this distance...

We went to the park and sat under a tree.

— So? Are you enjoying living there?

— It is all right.

— Are you eating well?

— They are good people, they call me for dinner, I do the dishes, all good.

— I had your laptop fixed.

— Can it be fixed?

— It does.

— That's good...

— Yeah... Thank God! That being said, you won't have a birthday present, and please control yourself. These attitudes don't help at all, they are only impairments. I don't even need to remind you when you broke the glass door with a punch to celebrate your football team's victory. Besides having to pay, you could have had a serious cut on your wrist.

I took some money out of my pocket and handed it to him.

— I still have some, I don't need it.

— Then save it for when you need it.

Not wanting to linger, he took the money and said goodbye.

I wanted to believe he was better. Maybe I just needed time for things to happen. The following week, I received a call from Cléber:

— Flávia, I wanted to talk about Davi.

My heart raced.

— What happened? — I asked scared.

— He's not trying hard to get a job, my son gave him some contacts, he did not go after it. We leave home early, come back after 3 p.m., he sleeps all day, gets up when we arrive...

— Cléber, Davi has depression.

— Oh, I suspected it... In this case, he'd better stay with you.

— I thought he was going to react in your house, have a new motivation, but apparently, it is not happening. A room is about to be vacant here, I wanted him to come back, focus on his goals, take the opportunity and study. He said he came back to take a College degree, but you know, he doesn't want to live with John.

— Don't worry, I will talk to him.

Once again, Davi arrived at the house unannounced, taking me by surprise.

103

We bought a snack around the corner and went to the park.

— How's the house? — he asked.

— Everything ok, same people.

— Are all the rooms occupied?

— One will vacate next week. The Portuguese woman is leaving. Why? Are you thinking of coming back?

— I don't know, I don't know.

— I have already told you a thousand times, Davi: your future depends on you. Life is not the way we want it, and sometimes we must swallow some frogs, or even many frogs, to conquer what really matters.

The conversation with Cléber had some effect, he was more confident and would return. On the eve of the Portuguese leaving, we had a farewell party. I called Davi, it would be a good time to meet the other young people. He agreed and asked me to pick him up and his suitcase. He said he would be okay on the living room couch for that night. Davi had a relaxed conversation with the Italian boys and John. "This could end well", I thought, happy.

That night would have ended peacefully if it were not for the conversations I heard from John with a friend over Skype during the party. John had already made some comments about his former co-worker. Among the lower tones of the music and the lively conversation in the room, I heard compliments from him to his friend that made me uncomfortable. One of those compliments being exaggerated and it hit me hard. I laughed at the boys, not understanding the joke, disguising the jealousy that burned me from the inside. After the party was over, I went to the room, John was already lying down. I could not control it. I quickly found ironic and harsh words, tasted like Kronenbourg beer, and poured over him.

From the living room, Davi heard the discussion and walked down the street in the middle of the night. I ran after him. I did not have time to find a slipper or close the door before Fred left, too.

— Davi! Davi! Come back, please, I am sorry, Davi, I could not control myself... I thought he was cheating on me. I don't know... I am lost...

Every couple has problems... Let us focus on our goals... I am going to focus on mine, you on yours... Everything's going to be okay.

He did not say a word. He kept walking towards the beach. I came home devastated. I went to Davi's room and laid down. He came back in the morning; I saw that he had posted on his Facebook pictures of the sunrise.

— Don't mind it, Davi, I know it is horrible, I should have waited for the right time to talk... I don't know what is going to happen between John and I, but I am strong now, I am with you. If we have to start over some-where else, we will, we're almost experts on the subject! I have to go out in the afternoon. Will you come with me? Let us go to College and see what the openings are for September?

The receptionist sent us to a room handing to Davi several informa-tive magazines about the courses. He was interest in few, but always put a huge obstacle in front it.

— Let's take the magazines home, you read, research on the inter-net, ask for opinion... There's still time to decide.

John had traveled and stayed away for two days. It was nice to calm down my thoughts and the house. When he got back, I entered the room; he was lying down, watching TV, serious, and ignored me. I walked quietly and sat by the bed.

— John, you have always respected me, one of the things I admire most about you is your faithfulness. You have never given me reasons to distrust you, I have always felt safe by your side, never had to look at your cell phone or investigate where and with whom you were. Yesterday I had my motives, I think you are cheating on me or interested in her. But... I abandoned you, didn't I? I left. I am feeling lost, confused...

— Nothing happened, Flávia, nothing ever happened. I wouldn't ruin our relationship like this, Lucy and I are just friends, it is no big deal. I was not faking it when I asked you several times to come back, I was not faking it when I said your place was here and that I loved you.

— I understand, John... And you? Can you understand?

He looked at me, sat on the bed and hugged me. I wouldn't insist on that. I know that sometimes there is an unexpected restlessness, a fury that passes by. I trusted him. Better to realign our steps and move on.

𝄢

Davi got all the documentation needed, filled out the forms, returned to the College, and enrolled in the business course. That was another gift he had. Ambitious, extremely dedicated in what he wanted, convincing, captivating, knew how to negotiate and had a leadership spirit. Said many times of becoming a businessman.

— I don't know if I made the right choice, I am not good at math.

— I think your difficulty in math has to do with that weak teacher you had in elementary school, remember? Our teachers have a big influence on our life. I failed in math during high school because of a stupid teacher, who kept criticizing me when I made mistakes. The next year, with a new teacher, I was one of the best students in class. You can reverse that. If you need to, you can take some private lessons, get out there and face it!

When Davi turned nineteen, he did not want me to do anything special, instead he just wanted to go to a nightclub with the two Italian boys. Before they left, we were in the living room with a couple of John's friends, the counselling ones. I saw Davi talking with them, I liked the approach. We made a toast to the birthday boy and they were excited to enjoy the evening. Two hours later, they were back. Davi had fought with a boy for a foolish reason. They exchanged punches and were kicked out of the club. A friendship with the Italians did not happen. Sometimes Davi would talk to Mike, an English friend of John's who was always around. When I asked him how College was, he would just answer that everything was fine. The second week I saw him in the kitchen at a time when he was supposed to be in College.

— Didn't you have class today?

— A boring one, I didn't go.

— You must go to the boring classes too, all classes! I don't want to see you skipping classes, you are going to study, do you understand, Davi?

— There's a teacher there who likes me very much. The first day, I asked him a few questions and he got carried away. My classmates respect me. At break time, my classmates and I were all in the room chatting about the subject we had learned. Nobody wanted to leave. The teacher said he'd never seen anything like that before.

— That is great, Davi. You found the right course! 'Knife on the skull'!

— But there are some dudes who just stare at me. I took the bus with one of them the other day. I am sure he kept watching me.

I did not like that. What was that paranoia about thinking people were staring at him?

— Don't mind the others, OK? It doesn't matter if they are looking at you or not. You are you, and that is it. Move on. You are getting along, you are enjoying classes, move on!

He kept spending a lot of time at home. I asked him if I could see the timetable of his classes, he got angry, said he was not a kid.

— You're not a kid and you are not going to skip classes because we have a deal and you are going to keep your end! — I told him almost shouting.

It did not help, he kept acting the same way.

— You're not dropping out of College again, are you?

— That isn't for me.

— What do you mean "it is not for you"? Yes, it is for you! Didn't you say you were doing great, that you impressed everyone?

— The teacher doesn't want me to leave at all, he even called me, but it is not for me, it isn't... You don't understand.

— No, I'm not understanding. What is the matter, then?

I had to force him, I could not let him give up again. I went up the stairs right behind him talking about what he promised me. He locked himself in his room, sleeping during the day instead of at night and started smoking pot again.

— It is easy! — said John. — Tell him to work and pay his bills, that is how it is done. Look at my kids! My kids are getting around by themselves!

Davi knew he could not stop again. I spotted him coming out of the house all dressed up. Around the corner, he met with Mike, exchanged a few words, said he was going to work at a restaurant downtown. On the second day of work, he came home early, did not want to talk. I texted a Brazilian friend who worked at the same restaurant, he told me that Davi simply quit the job, no one knew why.

— What happened, Davi?

— An Italian asshole. Told me to take out the trash. The first time, I did it. Then he sent me again just to provoke me. He could have asked someone else but asked me just to humiliate me. But I did it. Right after, he came and pat me on the cheek and told me, "Good boy." I pulled out my apron and left. No one humiliates me like that, asshole!

One night, John was in the dining room when Davi walked through the kitchen. John brought up the subject, wanted to know why he had left the restaurant. Davi explained, asked John not to comment with the Italians who were arriving at that time and went up to his room. I was right behind Davi when we heard John start explaining to the boys what had happened at the restaurant. Davi, who was already entering the room, suddenly turned to me pushing me aside and went downstairs furious.

— I will get this guy!

— Davi, don't do this! John! John!

Davi punched him in the face and walked out the front door. John didn't fight back; he didn't do anything. He was calm, took a selfie of the cut with a drop of blood dripping down his cheek and found it even funny. Then he asked me with an ironic tone:

— What will happen now?

— Nothing, nothing will happen now. He asked you not to comment about it, and you did not even wait a minute to talk behind his back.

— And is that a motive for him to punch me?

— And what were the reasons you freaked out the other day? The score is one to one, John! Game is tied! And don't forget you are the adult here.

Things were complicated. What was going to happen? Davi leaving the house again? No, it wouldn't work, I needed to keep him with me until the crisis passed, until he stabilized. When he came back, I went to his room so we could talk:

— You're smart, why act in such a stupid way? You showed such maturity that time when you asked me to take you to his house and reached out to him. A brilliant attitude of superiority! But now you do this?

— I could not control myself!

— You could not control yourself with your brother, at the club, and now with John. Do you need to unload? There is a boxing gym right here near home. Go there and get enrolled!

— No, I don't want to. Is John mad at me?

— No, he is not. He said it was a nice punch and even took a selfie of the cut on his cheek.

Davi laughed at John's reaction.

I thought I would get a full-time job and rent a small house for the three of us, Davi, Fred, and I but the idea of leaving him alone for long periods made uncomfortable. I felt like I was in a maze, with no way out. I needed to stay calm. A way out would come up. I would put up colorful flowers on the table, and open the windows on sunny days so light could get in.

In October, Bob, John's eldest son, and his girlfriend decided to spend a weekend with us. They lived in another city, where he attended university but was having bureaucratic problems and was waiting for a solution to get back studying. The two of them worked in a pub and shared a flat with some friends there. The rooms were occupied, they had to settle down in the small office. On Sunday, I didn't see any movement from them preparing for the return trip.

— Flávia, my son asked me to live here with his girlfriend.

— What do you mean? Is he not going back to the university?

— It seems it is not that easy.

— Did he lose his spot?

— I don't know for sure. It is depending on many things.

— John, we don't have room here, everything is occupied.

— I know, they know. They asked me to stay in the office. The job there is not easy, they earn badly, they cannot even pay all expenses. They have more options here.

— If they don't mind staying in the office...

Davi and Bob exchanged a few words in the early days. At another time, Davi greeted him, but it looked like Bob did not listen. Davi thought he did not want to answer and ignored the couple. When they met around the house, it was just an almost inaudible "hi". The couple made their own food, but Bob was always hungry. He kept wondering if he could eat what I had left in the fridge for Davi.

— Sure, feel free to take whatever you want.

At different times, everyone in the house prepared its own dinner, had its space in the kitchen's closet, in the refrigerator. It was like that in the other places I lived, but he was John's son, he was family.

— John, I'm embarrassed, I think I should cook for Bob and his girlfriend too.

— Don't worry, they can handle themselves. It is like this in here.

A few days later, John came up with another request from his son:

— Bob asked to change rooms with Davi.

— What do you mean?

— The office is too small for them.

— He knew that, didn't he? Besides, Davi's not here for free, re-member? I pay for his room, you know that.

When Davi returned the second time, I thought it was best for me to pay for the room and avoid future comments or demands. That smelled like intrigue. I did not accept or said anything to Davi. It's best if he doesn't know. The rooms were side by side, wall with wall. Davi continued to sleep a lot during the day and spent long periods on the computer. The couple, just so they bother him, turned on the vacuum cleaner and made other noises, complaining that they could not sleep at night because of him.

— Davi, you know that the walls and floors of these houses are very thin, it doesn't block noises. Then, don't stay up at night so you don't get in the way of other people's sleep, OK? Any news about work?

— I am still looking.

A few days later, John came to tell me:

— Bob and his girlfriend said the Italians are also complaining about Davi's noise at night.

I took advantage that the Italians were at home to investigate what Davi was doing that bothered them.

— No, Flávia, I hear no noise, Davi doesn't bother at all.

— But you did not complain to John's son?

— No, I did not complain to anyone. Complain about what?

I ran down the stairs and to talk to John:

— Can you clear this up for me please? There was no complaint!

John went to his son's room and came back saying:

— They admitted to making the story up.

— How beautiful! How old are they? How childish! I thought they were independent, mature. Isn't that what you always told me?

I started ignoring them, hoping they would get a job and another place to live. In the second week, the boy got a job as a salesman. Every morning his friend would call and let him know he was coming to pick him up. There was no exact time. A room freed up, and the couple moved in there. "It looks like they're going to be quiet now," I thought. The girl was also working a few hours a day at a neighborhood diner.

— Bob wants to change rooms with Davi — said John.

— Again? Isn't he in a room just for himself and his girlfriend? Why does it have to be Davi's room?

— Because the room where he is in, the cell phone signal is terrible. He needs to take a call every morning.

— And cannot he wait in the living room, as he is doing every morning? He is here as a favor and is making demands? When are you going to start paying his and his girlfriend's rent?

John did not want to argue about it. When I met Bob in the kitchen, I asked him why he could not take the calls in the living room. He rudely answered he was working while my son was not doing anything. He turned around and left. Mike was coming:

— Don't listen to him, Flávia, he is just a childish and jealous boy.

— I cannot tolerate it. I am leaving this house!

— Calm down, he is the one who must leave, not you.

Bob still wasn't satisfied, asked his father to do my desk job. John came up with his arguments:

— His job is not good; he is earning very badly.

— How weird, an English boy, university student, not getting a good job in his own country...

— I think it is best that my business stays in the family, he will learn a lot helping me.

— Great, John! I have not done anything anyway since he got here with his girlfriend. The office is a mess! I still have the house to run and I can get another job. I am glad Davi did not see anything, did not know anything, or we would have another problem. I just want to get out of here.

— You don't have to do that. It is all going to work out.

— You give in to all of your son's requests.

— And you let your son manipulate you.

— Davi is in trouble, he is not normal.

— Then go to the doctor.

At that point, Davi came to the kitchen, was fine, playing with Fred.

— Is everything all right? — he asked feeling something in the air.

— Everything OK, and you son?

— All good.

— Davi – asked John — the room Bob is in doesn't get a good cell phone signal, and he needs to take calls from his supervisor every morning. Can you change rooms with him?

— Yeah. It is not a problem. Wow! I have been through several rooms in this house!

Bob's office service with his father did not even begin. He did not get involved, he had no interest, and I totally walked away. Davi found a friend he had already worked with, she tried to fit him into the current restaurant.

— Davi, it would be great if you worked there, because the manager is moving to Scotland in May. If you could take his spot... I know you, you have the profile, you know how to talk to clients, solve problems. Remember that day we served 300 tables? And you still stood there at dawn helping close the register!

Davi had put in his head that he would wait until May to get the spot.

— Davi, it is a long wait! We are in December!

— Calm down, Mom, I need to be patient and wait, this is my chance.

— You need to find something else while you wait. You cannot be locked in your room all day waiting for May to arrive.

— If I find something else, I will lose my chance.

— No you won't! You just warn them, stop by, show that you are really interested, and they will call you!

— No, that is not how it works, you don't understand.

— You cannot use marijuana, Davi, it is not good for your head! It is just getting in your way, you are smart, how can you not see?

He started to scream:

— Get out of here! You broke me! Look what you've done to me! Look at me, look what I am today! It is your fault! Get out of here!

Sometimes he would come into the kitchen tense, giving orders.

— I am hungry. Where is the food?

Other times, he would come well, cheerful, singing, making plans.

— I am going to buy some pens! I want to make a panel on the wall of my room, all colorful! Have you ever thought about it, how cool would it be? And when people see it, they are going to ask me to paint their room too, and I make some money! I will even be in some magazines, have you thought about it?

— Wow, is your artistic gift back?

— Yes, but... What if no one likes it? What if it doesn't look good? What if I waste time on this and it doesn't work out?

— You won't know if you don't try.

No, no idea stood in his head for long. So, he returned to the isolation of his room. He once took the barbecue skewers that hung by the fireplace and struck the air as if he were a swordsman. Then he looked at them, passing his fingers through the thin ends.

— Would you like a smoothie? – I asked.

When he left the room, I took all the skewers and hid it under the rug behind the couch. I went to the health center to ask for help.

— My son has mental disorders, spends many hours locked in the room, his mind is not normal.

— How old is your son?

— Nineteen.

— He is of age; he must come on his own.

— He won't come on his own. Isn't there anyone who can go to our house?

— No, that is not how it works. You must convince him.

— He doesn't listen to me; he doesn't accept the idea that he needs to be treated.

— Keep trying — he turned his back on me, showing that he had something more important to do.

I waited for a moment where he was calm:

— Davi, I went to GP. You must fill out this form and take it there to make an appointment. It is near here...

— Stop being ridiculous. If you keep saying I am crazy, depressed, smoking pot, I am going to kick your ass!

— Don't talk to me like that, do you understand? You need treatment, Davi!

— Get out of here, leave me alone, leave me alone!

I heard people talking in the living room. They wanted me to take a radical attitude towards Davi, like kicking him out, because they understood the rude way, he had been treating me lately; they thought I was foolish to be patient with him. I searched the internet and called a highly known non-governmental organization about the human mind. I thought they were going to call me to talk in person, that they would want to listen to me, to know everything that was going on in detail, but no, they just advised me to take my son to the GP so he could be referred to a specialist. Sometimes John supported me, said he understood, other times, he didn't.

— If I am sick, I simply go to the doctor! But Davi doesn't, he refuses. " I won't go! I won't go! I won't go!". How do we solve that?

— That's what I am trying to figure out, John...

One night, I was in the kitchen washing the dishes when Davi arrived for dinner. He took a plate, served himself, put it in the microwave without saying many words, sat down at the table and began to eat. Suddenly he said, "You have a demon in your body. Not one, seven!" I looked scared, trying to understand the joke, but he was serious. I didn't say anything. I went to back to my room disoriented. John was there.

— What is it?

— I don't know... — I did not know if I tell him or not. I did. Mike saw me walk by and knocked on the door:

— What's going on?

— Davi said she has demons in her body — John replied.

— That's no reason to worry, everyone says that.

I preferred to let it go.

The next day, Davi was calm. Maybe it was really my impression, maybe he said that just to mock me, start an argument. Later, I was in the room, on the computer, with the door open when he approached.

— You never cared about me when I was in College.

— What do you mean?

— You never wanted to know what was going on with me.

— In College? What happened that I don't know?

— See? You don't even know what happened.

— I don't... Apart from those times where you did not know what course to take, I don't remember anything that important.

— I had the worst time of my life in that place. What I have been through there... And you did not even realize...

— You never told me anything about it.

— You're not attentive, you don't care.

— What happened?

— I suffered racism, racism from a colleague, a teacher... I was alone in there, and you don't even know.

— But that is a crime! You had to tell me!

— If you paid more attention, you would know.

— If I had known, I would have gone there immediately!

— Years like that, without being myself...

— Why didn't you ever tell me about it?

— Not even in my childhood problems you were present... The bullying I suffered in Brazil.

— You were always so independent, Davi, but everything that came to my attention, that needed my interference, I interfered, or else I had your father help. Remember your fights at school? Some people even think I do too much.

— You distort things. You always shift things your side. You play the victim; you don't understand anything. You ruined Joyce's, Israel's and my life. We were happy in that apartment in Belo Horizonte, you did not have to get us out of there.

— Davi, life was impossible, you don't know how hard I tried, all the problems, the traumas, the humiliations... I just wanted a better chance for you guys.

— You think it's beautiful to live in Europe... Look at the life you have, you have nothing! You ruined me. Look what I am today. I hate you!

I felt my body shudder, closed my eyes for a few seconds.

— Davi, you're not obliged to live with a person you hate. Davi, if I do you this bad, look at the world out there waiting for you...

— Now? Now that I am already destroyed?

— Destroyed, Davi?! You have so much potential, so many gifts! You only need to focus on one of them. Of my three children, you were the only one I didn't care about the future with because I knew you'd get along anywhere, in any area.

— Did you think that about me?

— I did and I have told you many times.

— You never told me.

— You don't listen… — "Why can't he remember?", I thought to myself.

— See, distorting things again! Shame on you!

— Look, Davi, if you want to stay here, you are going to have to respect me, do you hear me? If you don't want to, the front door is right there!

— I am not staying here, don't worry, I am not staying with you. I am getting out of this house.

Some things he talked about were distorted, others were not consistent with reality. If something so serious had happened at College, Bel, Israel or Joyce would have known.

I thought he was going to lock himself in his room again, but he left the house a few times. In one of them, he returned with a picture from the movie The Godfather. John was at home, quiet, listening to music, when he saw the painting in a corner of the room, he drew conversation with Davi about the film, which he also liked. It brought them closer again. That week, a friend of John's came to visit him. He knew my son was going through rough times. He was a successful businessman, with characteristics with which Davi liked to resemble. He agreed to talk to Davi. I went to get him in his room already waiting for a rude answer, but to my surprise, he went without complaining. John and I left them both alone. They stood more than an hour in the dining room. Stones hear too. Davi was living inside a rock.

On a Friday, late January, a lively party with some of John's friends was taking place at the house. Charlie, the owner, John's uncle, arrived too and, in that relaxed atmosphere, approached Davi, who was in the kitchen, and drew conversation. Two years earlier, in the little flat where John lived, Charlie and I talked about my kids. He wanted to know how they lived, what they did. At that time, he already knew from John that Davi was not happy with anything, that he wanted to work, and he couldn't get a job, he didn't like the courses offered by the College, he wanted to get a driver's license, but the insurance was too expensive and that he unloaded those frustrations on me.

— Leave it to me, I know how to handle situations like this. Tell him to call me, I will get him something.

I was moved by his interest in helping Davi. Charlie was a positive man, entrepreneur, fast minded, many contacts, owned many businesses and liked to help people — he was always campaigning for charities. It would be nice for Davi to become friends with him. Davi called two or three times. He did not pick up. I told John, "How weird, Charlie didn't answer Davi's calls." John immediately called his uncle, who gave an apology, said he was too busy and asked Davi to send him an e-mail. Davi did it. He never answered. After that, Davi no longer wanted to hear his name. When Charlie was going to visit us, Davi made a point of not showing up. That night, however, it coincided with the two meeting at a good time. I saw Charlie with his hand on Davi's shoulder outside the house, talking about his plans, and asked Davi to move a huge pile of bricks, paying a hundred pounds for the job. Davi accepted gladly, he needed the money, and it was a good restart with Charlie.

As people chatted excitedly in the living room and listened to music, I saw Davi and John in the kitchen, and I did not like it. There was a tense atmosphere. I called them both into the living room, Davi asked me to let them talk. I called Charlie, who went over there, asked if everything was okay, told a joke and came back to the living room telling me not to worry. The next time, I saw Davi punching John, and he fighting back. They both fell to the ground. Charlie separated them, Davi went up to his room and the party was over. This time, John got furious.

— I don't want Davi in this house anymore, do you understand, Flávia? He crossed the line! That is enough!

John would travel the next morning to France for work and wouldn't return for three days.

— All right, John, it is getting impossible to live together. Why don't you ask your son and girlfriend to leave as soon as possible, before your trip, please? I am not going to tolerate them in here for another day!

He did not answer.

I just stood there and cleaning up the mess. I did not realize Davi had left home. John was in the dining room, calmer, it was around 1 a.m. when I heard exalted voices outside. When I opened the door, I saw two policemen holding Davi, who shouted:

— Let go of me! Let go of me!

— What's going on? — I asked.

— Do you know this man? — asked one of the officers as the other immobilized him, holding his arm behind his back.

— He is my son!

Davi remained exalted:

— Why are you holding me? Is it because of my color?

— Does he ever come by? Do you have any entrances on the side of the house? — continued the policeman.

— Yes, we all use that entrance too. What is the matter?

— He did not stop at our command. We received call about a break-in attempt in the area and we are on the pursuit.

— This is racism! It is racism! — shouted Davi.

— He should have stopped at our command.

— You are right… He is just hot-headed…

— Why is that? Did he drink?

— Well, there was a fight in here about an hour ago.

— A fight? So, we need to register the incident.

John approached:

— No, no, no, it was just a family argument, no need register any-thing, no one was hurt.

— But you can take him, he is very exalted, and I think it is better for him not stay here tonight — I asked.

Davi got into the car in handcuffs shouting:

— Follow us, Mom! This is racism! Follow us!

Davi had this racism thing in his head. His brown skin and his father's traits grew on him an admiration for black people of strong personality. He watched movies, videos, and read articles on the Internet about his idols. On Facebook, he even changed his profile picture to one of a black actor. Later I found out that he was not an actor, but Frank Lucas, the mobster who inspired the movie American Gangster, which Davi watched several times.

John traveled the other day without saying goodbye. Few hours after, I heard people talking in front of the house. It was Davi and another man.

— Davi, what are you doing? — I asked.

— Charlie asked me to take out the bricks, and I am going to take it out.

— Davi, you better wait for this situation to calm down. It is not good for you to stay here today.

— Don't worry, I am not even going in, I am just here to do the job I promised Charlie. I brought a friend to help me.

They started carrying the bricks while I explained:

— Davi, Charlie is John's uncle, you fought with John, how do you think that is going to work out? He doesn't want to see you around here!

— Bring us a bottle of water and leave it outside at the door and a sandwich, I'm hungry.

— Davi, go to a friend's house until we figure out where we are going to live, OK?

— That's what I am going to do, but I promised Charlie, and I am going to keep my word first.

— Let it go! This job will take more than a day, it is not worth it! Are you going to kill yourself out here for twenty-five quid a day? You must share it with your friend!

— Charlie said a hundred pounds a day, that was the deal.

— No, it was not. I was there, I heard it, a hundred pounds for the whole job, regardless of how much time you spend.

— It is a hundred pounds a day! You can let me be in charge of demanding what he promised me.

I went to the kitchen worried. I had to fix that. A few moments later, I heard an argument outside. I ran to the door. It was Harry, John's other son, nervous, yelling at Davi, the two of them were staring each other closely.

— Did you punch my dad, huh? Did you punch him? — asked Harry infuriated.

Davi answered firmly, looking right into Harry's eyes:

— I did, so what?

I came in interfering, talking loudly to Harry:

— Who called you here? You don't know anything about what is going on!

Davi, without taking his eyes off him, told me to step away.

— I want to know who called you to fight Davi? — I continued.

Harry abandoned the discussion and entered the house, went upstairs looking for his brother. I walked in right away, picked up the phone and went into the living room to call John, outraged:

— I asked you to get your son out of here before you left, and you did not do anything!

— I want to know what Davi is doing in there — he asked in the same tone.

— He came to do the job Charlie asked him to do, while your dissimulated son sits there in the room with that girl, architecting coward plans, using his own brother to fight Davi, comfortably watching the circus catch fire.

— I want Davi out of there now!

— I want your son and his girlfriend out of here now, or I will call the police!

I went outside and asked Davi and the boy to leave. When I got back, I met Harry in the kitchen. He had grown up, he was a sensible boy, honest, had true feelings.

— Are they going to your house? — I asked.

— Yes, they're getting some things... Jesus Christ, what is happening here?

121

— Harry, Davi is not well.

— Yeah… I saw it in his eyes...

When I was about to would explain it better, the girlfriend, very thin and delicate, appeared at the door holding a knife and cursing several swear words. That attitude did not suit her. She was polite, complacent, but she was totally dominated by her boyfriend. I stood there, watching the scene and just said coldly:

— *Au revoir, mademoiselle.*

A month earlier, John and I went to visit another house that his uncle Charlie had bought to expand his English school. It was a big house, incredibly good, but we did not want to live temporarily again. I suggested John to get the house and leave it to his son and his girlfriend to manage. Then, they would leave my life without problems. He would think about it.

John arrived from France serious and with sudden movements, throwing the little suitcase on top of the bed.

— Davi is not here, is he? — he asked aggressively.

— No, and neither is your son and his girlfriend. I think you'd better take that house and move in with them. We cannot get along anymore, John. Each one with its own problems.

I left him alone. I went to Davi's empty room and we did not talk anymore. That same week, he arranged for most of his furniture to be removed and moved out. Davi went to Alan and Leticia's house, a couple of friends. He enrolled in the boxing academy and went out a few times to hand out resumés. I called my friend:

— How is he, Leticia?

— He is all right, Flávia, he only sleeps a lot and spends many hours on the Internet, but he's a good boy, helpful, polite, don't worry. What he lacks, in my opinion, is a father reference.

I crossed my fingers so that Davi would work with her husband, a great guy, very dynamic and had many Brazilian friends. They were always having barbecues on the weekends. But there was no vacancy in the small business, and Davi could not stay in their house for long, for it was already full.

One night, John went to the big house to pick up some of his belongings and use the internet to finish a job. I didn't want to be in his presence. I borrowed the car to go to the supermarket and went to meet Davi.

— I need a place to live, I cannot get a job. Damn it! Damn it!

— You had a place to live, didn't you, Davi?

— I wish I had broken him up!

— Oh, how beautiful, to ruin your life like that? Think bigger, Davi, think about your projects, your future, don't give a damn about these things, if you keep on going like this you won't move. You can't get work because you're too loaded with these negative emotions, people want happy people, you can't concentrate because of this depression and you don't want to treat yourself, life doesn't respond positively!

— Is he still in the house?

— He's there at the moment, but he already moved out. I am renting the room that was ours for a man who's a children's soccer coach — I was looking for every fact to see if something touched Davi.

— What about you? Where are you going to stay? — he asked.

— I will go to the office, so I save a little money.

— What about my room?

— It is there, Davi, but for you to come back, you need to be by my side. There is no John in the story anymore. We have to take advantage of the little time we have in the house to organize our lives.

Davi returned to the big house, and a few hours later, I got the call from Charlie wanting to talk. From his tone of voice, the conversation would be difficult. Mike had already spread the news. Charlie entered the house with rush:

— I know Davi is back.

— Yes, he is.

— This is my property and I don't want any trouble in here. He has done enough! Even the police were at the door!

— Charlie, Davi is not well.

He turned his eyes and shook his head mockingly, as if to say "Oh, don't give me that nonsense!", and continued giving orders that I did not listen; I got up, feeling the angry words preparing to attack, and interrupted him:

— Yes, he is and has been in trouble, for a long time, it is getting worse and worse, and what have you done for him? Nothing! You told him to call you, to email you, and you never even answered! Do you remember that Charlie?

— Where is Davi? Go get him Davi, I'll talk to him!

— He's not at home.

— He doesn't want to face the situation, right?

I repeated it louder and slower:

— He-is-not-at-home! He went out to look for work.

— Look, Flávia, I have a lot of consideration for you, but please, I don't want any trouble again, do you understand me? There won't be any next time.

—Thank you, Charlie — I answered dryly.

Chapter 11

The next two and a half months were a lot of work. Ever since I lost my role as John's secretary, I got back into dedicating to the research about indigenous people. I had submitted a proposal to an educational organization in London to hold an event in April. The Brazilian Embassy gave us the place and we set the date. The small office became even smaller with the pictures on the wall, the texts and the ideas that arose.

Davi was more excited. He cleaned his room, the fireplace, and went out from time to time to look for work or go for a walk. One night he came home with two bottles of pepper.

— I met a guy who sells Brazilian products. He took me to his house just to get the pepper I wanted. He is a good guy, we were having a super interesting chat, so he asked me how old I was. When I told him I was nineteen, he did not believe me, he thought I was about twenty-four. After that he did not talk to me anymore.

— Oh, Davi, what do you mean?

— Seriously, he did not talk to me anymore. — It should have been the opposite, don't you think? Anyway, don't give a damn, it might have been just an impression of you.

A few days later, he quit boxing and fell into depression again. I tried to change the curtains in his room, put on a more cheerful color, but he did not want to. I would call him for a walk with Fred, tell him about the man who did physical activities on the park's equipment, kept looking for ways to make him react — nothing worked. This time it was even worse, he was sadder, more immersed in his lonely world and without prospects.

— Can you help me? — he asked me with anguished air.

— On what?

— I am going to spend a year traveling.

— Where to? With whom?

— Alone. I don't know where yet. Lots of places. I will stay for a while in one place, then another... I will get some work, but I need some support, only you can give it to me.

— But alone is very lonely...

— Who would go with me? I have no one. You need to stay here to help me. So, I am going alone.

That hurt... I understood what he wanted: peace. To live without pressure, without charges, because they were killing him little by little. Just live. I was not afraid of losing him to a free world, I was afraid of losing him to his own sick world.

— Let us think about this possibility... Let's think about it calmly, okay?

When I worked at the hospital, I once talked to a nice mental health assistant, where I cleaned every night. I told him about the problems that were going on with Davi. He lived in London at that time.

"It is difficult at this age to distinguish what is a problem from what is rebellion. But if you think he is really in need of medical attention, look up in your neighborhood for a GP, they'll guide you."

I remembered this conversation and decided to go back to the GP, only this time I would talk to a doctor, not someone from the reception, as I did before. I made an appointment, and after reporting some of Davi's symptoms, she asked:

— How old is he?

— Nineteen.

— He's of age, he needs to make an appointment so we can make an appraisal.

— He won't accept...

— You must try to convince him, or have a friend to try, perhaps.

— He doesn't listen to anyone. He is already talked about killing himself.

— When he says that, call the police, they know how to act. Keep trying, eventually you will make it.

She got up, ending the appointment.

𝄢

I was gathering things on the table, it was already late, I was about to lie down when Davi showed up in.

— Are you, all right? — I asked.

He pulled out a chair and sat down. I opened a cardboard box, took out the brushes, a sponge, the paints, and stood there, giving him the opportunity to talk. There was a door between the dining room and the visitors' room where I was painting, making some stains, and everyone could write or paint whenever they wanted.

— Would you like to paint? – I asked.

He took the brush, wet it in black paint, went to the door and wrote:

"Somebody or nobody."

— What do you mean by that?

— It is a quote from a movie. "Somebody or nobody."

— Davi, why don't you get your driver's license and get a part-time delivery job, just a few hours, what do you think? You like driving so much!

— It is too expensive to get a license.

— I can help you.

— No, it's too expensive, too expensive...

I suffered seeing that lost look in his eyes, desolated, joyless, unmotivated, seeing in the small difficulties unsurpassable barriers that were making him give up everything he liked the most. I had to do something to get him back. I opened the laptop and started looking for a car to buy.

— The good thing is that cars are cheap in here — I said.

— But insurance is expensive.

— If we work, we will be able to pay!

He did not care, distanced himself, and went to his room. I kept looking and wrote down on paper two offers that I found interesting. I asked him to call and make an appointment so we could check the cars. He did not. The next day, when I called, the cars had already been sold.

— Good car sells fast, we must keep an eye on the ads and have the money in hand to close the deal quickly — I told him, but he did not say anything.

I was in my room, talking on my phone, something about the event. He came in and stood around, tried to get in my laptop, wanted to see my conversations, read my messages.

— Don't go through my stuff!

— I need money to buy the car.

— Davi, that is not how it works, not in that tone, demanding, "I need this or that", don't give me orders.

— All right. I found a car on the Internet and made an appointment for tomorrow. If it is good, I will close the deal.

— I cannot go tomorrow. I must go to London.

— But I already made an appointment with the guy, I don't want to miss the opportunity.

— Then get someone to go with you.

— I will try… People are usually working at that time....

When I got back from London in the late afternoon, he came to tell me that he had closed the deal and asked for help filling out the vehicle transfer form. He was very interested and committed to it. For the first time after many months, I could see a way out in that look. He already had a provisional driver's license. Next day, I bought the apprentice plates, got the insurance on the Internet and went out for the first ride. It was a sunny Saturday in April. He drove on a long road, on a small seaside road to the south of the country. We went into a village and stopped at a pub for a refreshment. When we returned home, I called him for a serious conversation:

— Davi, now you need to go after your permanent driver's license. Before getting it, you are not going to drive this car without me by your side. I'm not going to be teaching you anything because you drive better than me, but you know the country's laws very well, you know you can't drive unaccompanied by a driver who has a British driver's license for at least three years. Now, take this car and turn your life around, got it?!

— Thanks, Mom, for giving me the money for the car – he said while giving me a hug that I thought was a little cold hearted but had a huge meaning. My feeling was that I had hit the target and that now he would have every reason in the world to react positively.

It was three days before the event at the Embassy, and I still had a lot to do. My head was loaded. On Sunday, Davi sat on the living room couch to watch TV, which he rarely did because he avoided meeting people. That afternoon, there was no one at home. I decided to make a chicken pie for lunch. When I approached him with the plate and a glass of juice, he took his eyes off the television, looked at me strangely, furious, and said:

— You must be taken down a peg or two!

I shivered, put the plate and glass on the table and spoke with my voice choked:

— You need a doctor.

He got up, I took a few steps back and tried to push him away with my hands; he held my arms and slapped my face.

— You cannot do this to me, I am your mom!

He locked himself in his room and I left the house, crying, walking aimlessly. On a street corner, I met Ludvik, an incredibly good boy from the Czech Republic who had been in the house for a couple of months.

— What happened Flávia?

— Davi slapped me...

— Take it easy, let us go home, don't just walk around like that.

— I don't know what to do, Ludvik. How am I going to meet with him? He is out of his mind! Why did he do that?

129

— Let us go home. I am going to try to talk to him. If you need me, just call, I will be in my room.

Ludvik knocked on his door, nothing. Called, he did not answer.

I slept very badly and woke up around six o'clock in the morning with unbearable pain on the right side of my chest. I had complained about this pain to Joyce a few times, she advised me to see a doctor, but I did not. That morning, though, I could not move. I called the ambulance. They went to the house and took me in for some preliminary tests. Davi came to see what was happening.

— Do you want him to stay here with you? — asked the paramedic.

— No... — I answered with fear, looking at him.

Davi got away, annoyed by my answer. I was visibly stunned, the paramedic asked me what was going on. I told him

— Would you like us to direct you to the Social Assistance department?

— Yes, please, I really need help.

I was taken to the hospital. The tests did not show anything concerning. Right after, the social worker showed up, very polite, listened everything calmly and advised me to call the police.

— No, I am not calling the police.

— Flávia, he assaulted you, he needs to know that this is very wrong. If he doesn't stop now, the situation could get worse.

— He's out of himself, he is not normal.

— Then he needs to go to the doctor.

— He refuses to go, won't accept even talking about it.

— Making a police report, he will be ordered not to approach the house anymore.

— So, after jail I am going to throw him out on the streets?

— Flávia, it is not you; he is the one doing this to himself. He is not going to be thrown out on the streets, he is going to get all the help he needs to start his life over.

— Governments aid? He is not going to take that kind of help.

— Someone will be there to guide him; he needs to find his own ways. He is an adult.

— He needs treatment!

— If the police think he needs treatment, he will be directed to it.

— What if they find he doesn't?

— Certain information obtained by the police are confidential, but I will keep you informed of everything I can.

I went home with that 'pain cutting through the meat': calling the police for my own son... A criminal? A sick man? Both together? No... No... Was that the only option? When I came into my room, I saw the broken mirror on the floor.

— Davi, did you break my mirror?

He came out of his room shouting:

— What I wanted was to break your face! Look, there is nothing, is there? There is no heart problem! Liar! Victim!

I picked up Fred, went to the corner of the street and called the police.

Behind the tree leaves, consumed by a pain that ripped away from me the images of him as a child, my endless struggle to put him in a safe place in life, crying, sobbing, bleeding, I saw him leave the house in hand-cuffs and get into the police car.

"What's happening to you, my son?"

I went into his room. On the computer, violent scenes from a movie and, next to it, half bottle of vodka. An hour later, a police officer arrived to get my statement. Mike had asked to stay in the house for a few days while he was looking for a place to live. When he got home from work, he saw the uniformed officer in the living room and went up to his room. I couldn't hide it. Later he came down to talk and said to me:

— This won't get anywhere. Here in this country, this is going to be understood only as violence against women.

— No, it is not possible, they must help him, he needs treatment.

I thought about who could approach him to give some direction, offer some friendship, a support. If I talked to any of his friends, he would revolt even more against me. Besides, none of them knew what was going on. He needed the help of a firm, neutral adult. But who? One time while I talked to a friend, she told me about Antonio, a Brazilian pastor who was back in town and who once played soccer with Davi. He was the ideal person. I found out his phone number and called.

— Antonio, we don't know each other, but I know you have played soccer with my son, which can be a great way to approach him. He really needs help.

I reported the facts, apologized for looking for him without ever going to his church, and cried out to him to go to the police station, because it would be the best place to talk to Davi.

— Don't worry, I will do anything I can to help you.

I had to focus and finish the mural for the event the next day. I was very late, I spent long hours working at dawn. I almost did not sleep, I wanted to give up. I thought of the people involved who too dedicated themselves so much, the children... I got up, took a shower, got the material and went to London.

At the Embassy, anxious about the latest preparations, I received a call from the police saying that Davi would be released in an hour and that he was forbidden to return home. "Released? Already?" — I did not have time to think about what he has done. The event was about to begin.

The hall was beautiful, colored with photographs of people of various ethnicities. The children heard stories and asked many questions to the indigenous guests from northern Brazil. Adults also took the opportunity to get to know a little of their culture. I felt fulfilled that everything worked out in the middle of that storm.

I went home thinking where Davi would be..."Did Antonio go to the police station?", "Why did they release him so early?", "Did they have time to do some psychological investigation?". I sent Antonio a message:

— Were you able to talk to him?

— I have not had a chance yet. Don't worry, I will keep you posted.

When I got home, I went to the kitchen and encountered Davi.

— Davi, you cannot come in here — I said in fear.

He was leaning against the sink, he looked quiet, his arms resting crossed.

— I have nowhere to go. You brought me here, you put me in this situation.

I was not going to start any conversation at that time of night.

— There's food in the fridge. Eat, take a shower and rest. We'll talk tomorrow.

I left the house, called a taxi and went to a small hotel in the neighborhood. When I came back the next day, Mike was home. He did not greet me, and said right away:

— No one wants Davi here.

I heard that in astonishment. He had spent hours the night before talking about Davi's situation in a tone of understanding and friendship, and now he is saying that? I asked:

— No one who? You, right? Because Ludvik doesn't care, the Italian, much less, there is no one else in the house, so 'nobody' is you! Why don't you just leave?

I could not stand another underhanded person at that point of the latest events. That wasn't the first time. He had already been intrusive, as soon as John left the house, he made an inappropriate comment and we had a disagreement. Later, he recognized that I already had too many problems, apologized to me, said he would soon find a place to live, but stayed there, trying to be helpful, a friend, went with Davi a few times to the corner pub, gave good advices. Davi liked him, he liked to hear his stories about archeology. I would be relieved if I didn't have him around. I needed people by my side who could help, not the other way around.

After spending hours in the room, Davi came to talk to me

— You cannot stay here, Davi, you have a police order.

— I have nothing, I have no job, I have no home, I have no one.

— Because you don't want to! I did everything I could. You cannot stay here, you assaulted me.

— It was not to hurt you.

— It doesn't justify! This is serious. It is so serious, that you could not even be here.

— I just want to get a job and buy my ticket to Brazil. That is all I am asking you, to stay here until I get it.

— You cannot give any more trouble, Davi. None!

— I am won't give you any trouble.

— It's a promise, right?

— Yes.

— You must apologize to me.

— I am sorry.

— You cannot say it just for the sake of saying it. It must be from heart, with regret.

— I am sorry.

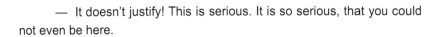

I had an appointment with the social worker that day. I told her Davi was back.

— Flávia, that is not good. I know, it is your youngest son, you want to do your best, but you are at risk. It is likely that everything will happen again, and you need to be prepared. We are going to help you.

— Help me? I don't need any help! He needs help! Him, not me!

— He's of age, he must seek his own help.

— My God, he is sick... Doesn't anyone understand that? What about the police? Did they investigate anything about his illness? Got a doctor, a psychologist, a psychiatrist while he was in custody, because out here it is impossible to convince him. It had to be inside, but nothing seems to have happened. No one came to me to ask anything!

— I am sure he's got all the information he needs, Flávia.

— And what does a person with mental disorders do with a lot of information?

— Do you want to go to a refugee home? It is not good for you to be around him.

134

— What?

— It is a safe place. He must be very angry that you called the police and might want revenge. Usually, that is what happens.

— No, I don't want to.

— Do you feel safe at home? Does your room have a key? Are you alone during the day?

I was airborne, automatically answering the questions, trying to understand them, mixing them with other questions that came to mind as she taught me techniques to prevent an attack.

At home, I sat on my bed staring at everything that was happening in desolation... On the computer, emails about the event I needed to answer, texts to write. I turned it off and lay down. Davi knocked on the door:

— Come to my room so we can talk.

— Davi, these conversations are not doing any good for you and neither for me. You insist on blaming me...

— You insist on running away, you don't want to face the truth, you are not humble, you don't recognize that you make mistakes, you have a problem, you are unbalanced. You are the one who should have had treatment. What could happen to a son of an unbalanced mom? You ruined everyone's lives.

I realized later that Davi had fixed in his mind lines he heard in childhood, fights he witnessed between his father and me. He was not being able to discern the past and present. Confusion of feelings, distortion of reality, speeches, accusations spoken in the heat of discussions that he absorbed as true. I got a piece of paper and a pen.

— Let's talk. I am going to write everything down, so it is clear what each of us is saying, no distortion, come on.

He got a little scared, started talking, and I, writing, but he got angry.

— No one can stand you, my poor father, who endured you for so long. If it were Alberto in this situation, he had already killed you by now.

I was shocked. I got up and walked quickly to my room. I opened the computer and sent a message to his father, accusing him. Alberto is one of his best friends. He replied that he was unaware of what was going on, that he never heard of it. I did not know if it was true or not, but, anyway, it was there, carved in Davi's head.

The next morning I saw him leaving the house elegant, as he liked to be, wearing khaki pants and a white shirt, with rolled-up sleeves, beautiful watch and shoes on, which were from nice brands, that he bought when he was working. I was getting ready to walk with Fred when he came into the house, nervous, talking loudly, giving orders. He wanted me to drive him somewhere at that exact moment. I saw it was nothing urgent. I calmly said, "That's not how you ask for things," and I left.

When I came back, I went up to my room and saw him from the window come through the gate, still nervous, yelling at me, arrogantly. I ran halfway down the stairs and said, "Don't talk to me like that!" He came up the stairs towards me. I ran into my room screaming, "Don't come near me!" I closed the door. There was no lock, just an improvised rope I had put up. I held the door with my body while he kicked.

— I'm calling the police! — I screamed

He stopped kicking, but he'd already drilled a hole in the door. I heard him say, "Look what you've done! I was already going to work..."

The police came, he tried to talk, I saw everything from the window. He told the cops they did not need to handcuff him, that he'd go to the police station without the slightest problem. A policewoman came up to my room to report the incident. I told her again about the mental disorders that were affecting him. She took some pictures of the broken door.

— Please help my son, he is not well, he is having some strange attitudes, he is not normal.

— Does he have any kind of paranoia? — asked the policewoman.

— Yes, he has symptoms of paranoia and other disorders. He refuses to go to the doctor. Please do something.

— We will do what we can.

I thought this time they would send him for an evaluation with a psychiatrist. I called the social worker telling her.

— It seems they have figured it out now. That's good — she said.

I also called Antonio, the pastor.

— Please, Antonio, he has been arrested again, go down to the station and talk to him...

— We have a service tonight, but tomorrow I will think of something.

— He won't be able to come back here. Please get him a place, I will pay for the room, he needs a place where someone can give him support, where he can find some aid.

— Yes, I am going to look for a place.

— I have no one to ask for help, Antônio...

— Don't worry, we will figure it out.

The next day, I got the call from the police informing that he would be released and that he was forbidden to go near the house, he could only pick up his belongings accompanied by a police officer.

— Did he get any assistance to assess his mental problems? – I asked.

— This information is confidential.

— I am his mom!

— He's of age, I am sorry.

It seemed that they were not considering my statements and that those police reports were only incriminating him more. I called the social worker.

— I want to know if they made any evaluations while he was in custody.

— I don't have that kind information, Flávia.

— But if the police cannot force him to a diagnosis, a treatment, who can? He's loose from the police station again. What was the help? No one can tell me!

— Who can determine whether he gets treatment, now, is the judge. A hearing will be scheduled, and if he understands that Davi needs treatment, he will force him. That is the way. Only the judge has that power.

I was terribly distressed and dissatisfied with the direction things were going. An audience... Me accusing a son that I love, who I know is sick, and my son, on the other side, accusing me, without any medical help, and a judge to draw conclusions, or not, that Davi might be suffering from mental disorders. A judge is not a doctor! Why all this suffering? What would be going through Davi's mind, who already had so many afflictions, that no one was able to hear, to know, let alone to understand? How it eroded me from the inside, how much cruelty and despair had that situation in which we were placed.

137

Chapter 12

Looking through the window, I saw that his car was not in front of the house, where I left it. I called a friend, Luisa. I heard she helped him get his last job, the same friend who pointed us to that room in London. I told her we had a fight and he left home.

— I know... He told my friend he was being held at the police station.

— He's going through a rough patch; I don't know where he is.

— Looks like he slept in the car.

— Do you know of any place he can stay at?

— There's an empty room in the house I live in, but it's too expensive. Five hundred pounds a month.

— It would be nice if he could be close to you, Luisa, he trusts you. He needs someone who can help him. Please tell him that you are lending the rent money and that you are not in the slightest hurry to get it back. He cannot know I am paying. Then you guys create one more bond, it's easier for him to listen you. You know, Luisa, he needs to go to the doctor.

— I got it, Flávia, I will help you. But he is not going to bring me any trouble, is he?

— No, his problem is with me...

Sometime later, I got the call from the social worker.

— Flávia, I want you to think about the possibility of going to the refugee home. Your son didn't respect the police order the first time, it's likely he won't respect it now either. I just found out there's a spot right here in town. Can I get it for you?

— You can...

She was right; it was not hard to predict the consequences. Arresting him fueled the hatred against me. We were ambushed... Now they can play the beautiful role of protecting me from the claws of a marginal young man. Trapped in a maze. My son and I lost in nefarious ramblings, victim of his debilitated mind, struggling with himself to cling to some of his remaining normality. The person I love so much so close to killing me.

I told the people at the big house I was going to spend a few days with a friend that had just got out of the hospital. That way, I wouldn't have to keep explaining my absence. Davi used his cellphone to send messages cursing at me of all the horrible names he knew. At the refugee women's house, I received instructions, the room key and a paper with the time and names of the social worker and psychologist who would see me the next day. I looked at all of that thinking about my son. What reversal of reality was that? Leave in absentia who needs help the most. Who am I for them to listen? An ignorant, Third World immigrant. Over there, they knew how to do the right things.

I declined the appointment with the psychologist, asking to speak only to the social worker.

— I called the police and filed the police report hoping that my son would be referred for treatment, which did not happen. I don't agree with the hearing being scheduled for me to accuse my sick son. I want to know what other way for us to solve this problem.

— Don't worry, you won't come face to face with him, you don't even have to go there. Your statement can be taken from here, through a camera.

— Don't you get it? He is sick. Nobody wants to hear me. He has never been diagnosed, he refuses to go to the doctor, he refuses the idea of having a disease.

She then wrote down on a paper the email address of the Mind organization and suggested that I get in contact with them.

— I have already talked with them. They want Davi to go to the GP to be diagnosed. That didn't work.

— Wait a minute, please.

She left the room and returned minutes later with a few pages she had printed, a text titled Mental Health Act 1983. She turned at me in saying that in there I would find the information I needed. It was the law applied in the UK on the care and treatment of people diagnosed with mental disorders, "and they may be detained in hospital or police custody and have their disorder assessed or treated against their will."

— I have read it on the Internet. This law only applies for people who have been diagnosed. Thanks for trying...

I remembered the cop in my room taking pictures of a broken old door and a cheap mirror. That was seen only as property damage. They did not take into consideration what I said about his invisible illness. They ignored my requests. I felt used, only to incriminate him.

I called a Brazilian organization in London, had to find help from my country. The lawyer who answered me on the phone just repeated what I was tired of hearing:

— He's of age, he must answer for his actions.

— He's not well mentally...

— So, the judge will determine if he needs treatment.

Of course, she knew the British laws and the system very well. I did not have the emotional condition to continue the conversation. No hope.

The letters about the hearing began to arrive. Davi continued to insult me through his cell phone messages. The fear that I had of him thinking about suicide again never abandoned me, from the first time he spoke, and it had increased now. I called Luisa every day to ask how he was doing. She worked a lot, she had little free time. She would go home practically just to shower and sleep, which meant that the contacts between them were short.

— He's fine, Flávia, I always step in his room when I arrive, and we talk a little. I don't see anything wrong with him, he is polite and helpful. All he needs to do is focus on work.

In a message, Davi told me he had been fired, but I figured out that he resigned. He was getting more and more pressured. On the outside, he struggled to survive in a society full of demands and, inside, he fought with an invisible monster that destroyed him, which left him blind, deaf, without paths. I imagined the hours he would spend alone trying ways out, desperate escapes. He needed to turn the tables, fool his monsters, get out of the line of fire, let his army fight for him while he rested and recovered. If he could understand that... It was asking a lot, I know, but with no options I had to try again.

— Davi, everything will be fine, I am in contact with some Brazilian lawyers in London who will help you. Everything can be solved faster and easier if you just say that you are going through many problems in your life, that you are not well mentally, emotionally... Davi, this is not the end of the world, our mind gets sick too, a lot of people have this problem. Some people don't but say they do just to justify some thoughtless act — he hung up.

I asked his father to come to Brighton to give him some comfort, distract him, but he thought it was not necessary, for Davi would return after the hearing. Besides, he did not have a passport or money for the trip. I picked up the letter on the table with the day and time of the hearing, and I called the contact number.

— I need to talk to someone about my son's mental health problems urgently.

They arranged a call with another social worker. I told her the whole case. I could not stand to hear that anymore:

— Only the judge can force you son into treatment.

— Why only the judge? Is the judge a doctor? Why didn't they subject him to an examination when he was arrested? Two, three times arrested! Would you like to be in court against your sick son? Is this the only way out?

— Flávia, I understand your affliction, but that is the only way under the law.

— No, you don't understand my affliction!

— Look, do you authorize me to accompany you to the hearing? I can talk to the people present before it starts, explain to them your situation. "That is better than nothing," I thought.

That night, I did not go to the refugee home. I decided to sleep in the big house. I was at the computer around 1:30 a.m., when I received a message from Davi:

— Come down and so we can talk. — I got scared, jumped out of bed, and went to the window; I pulled the curtain and saw the car standing in front of the house.

— I am not well. I had mouth surgery today, I cannot talk — I lied.

— It won't be long.

— Tomorrow.

— Ten minutes, for fuck sake.

— I have a fever. Leave.

He drove out burning tires.

It was late for a conversation. Where would he have been before? Drinking? Smoking? The next day at 7:30 a.m. I woke up with a horn ringing uninterrupted, deliberately bothering the neighborhood. It was him. I texted: "Go away, we can't talk with you like this." No talking like that. Did he spend the night on the street to be here so early? I had to find a way to take his car from him. Half an hour later, he called:

— The police took my car, it was your fault, you wouldn't listen to me.

— What happened?

— I hit a transit sign. You must go there to get the car

— If it is too damaged, it is not worth paying to get it back. — I was relieved and wouldn't go to pick it up, just so I would get rid of that problem.

— It is not, it just scratched. I am going to get you so we can go there.

— I cannot today, I am sick because of the surgery.

— My wallet and keys to the house are in the car.

— Go there and get it, they are your belongings, you have the right to pick them up and let them know that when your mom gets better, she will pick up the car.

In another message, he said he had seven lawsuits on court. I figured they would be related to the car: one, was driving without a license; two, hit the sign; three, escaped from the site; four, the address of the provisional license was not up-to-date, which is also a misdemeanor. Five and

143

six would be the times I called the police. I could not think of the seventh, I thought he had done the math wrong.

— Close to eight, they almost got me the breathalyzer test, I had already drunk two beer cans.

— Stop screwing up, Davi! You are screwing up one after another! What are you getting out of it?

— Dirty record, nineteen years old, fucked up in life.

— We can work all this out.

Two days later, I went back to the big house to take Fred for a walk. When I turned the corner, I saw Davi walking halfway down the small block towards me. When he saw me, he downed his face like he could not stand my presence and said something, probably a bad word. I walked back a few steps across the street to be strategically more visible on the corner, as I had learned. He thought I was leaving and shouted:

— Wait, wait, don't leave!

— I am just going to stay here so I don't get in the way of people passing by.

— Let us go get the car now.

— I'm not going...Look at how you are!

— I am not even going to look you in the face, I just want you to get the car out of there.

— Davi, let us go to a church, so you can calm down...

— Stop being ridiculous, you have fucked everything! – started cursing at me, completely out of his mind. I walked to the door of the first house and rang the bell, would ask for help to make a call. I was very nervous. No one answered. He crossed the street and stood in front of me, cursing. When he saw my cell phone in my hand, he left. I called the ambulance.

— Please, I need an ambulance now, my son is mentally ill, please! Mental Health Act 1983!

— Is he hurt?

— No. He is not normal.

— Where are you?

— On the street, near home.

— Is he in there with you?

— No, he just turned the corner.

— Can you see him?

— No. I am afraid of him.

— We cannot come if he is not in there. You need to call the police. When the police stop get him, we will go.

I called the police, who arrived in two minutes.

— Please find my son, he is mentally ill, I called the ambulance, but he was already gone. You need to stop him, but I don't want the police to take him in, I want the ambulance!

The policemen went out with the descriptions I gave them. Said they would be in touch when he was found. They didn't find him.

The next day, I got a message from Davi: "Do you want to know what happened to the car? Go there find out!" I figured they destroyed it, that is what they were doing in those cases. I did not care at all: "Material things we can buyback, Davi. You must take care of your health."

I asked his father, by email, to urge Davi to go to the doctor, to accept his mental disorders. I believed that this way he wouldn't have to go through the stress of the audience and that it would relieve his tension.

Joyce warned me that she got a message from him asking for money.

— Joyce, tell him to get the money "you" are sending at Leticia and Alan's house. I am going to leave the money there now. It is a way to get him out of the house, talk to other people, get distracted.

He did not go. He called me singing ironically:

— The little boy is hungry; he has nothing to eat.

— Didn't you get the money Joyce sent you?

— I am not going. I am going to stay here and starve to death. I don't even have the money to pay for a bus ride.

— It is hard for me to help you seeing the way you treat me. I am going to transfer an amount to your account now so you can eat and pay for the bus. Tomorrow, you get the money at Leticia's.

Chapter 13

I decided to spend another night at the big house to take care of Fred. The next day, Saturday, I woke up at eight in the morning and saw a message from Davi on my cell phone: "I'm not a sucker."

I looked at the time it was sent, 3:30 a.m. I went into the kitchen to make a coffee and think of good, positive words to say to him when someone knocked at the door. As always, Fred made a point of warning in high tone. It was two police officers.

— Are you Davi Pereira's mom?

— Yes, I am — I answered worriedly. — What happened?

— Can we come in and talk?

— Of course, please come in.

As they entered the room and I tried to calm Fred down, which was still barking, I thought, "Did they finally come to talk about Davi's problem? But this is not the time... They should have warned me..." Before they sat down, one of them said: "Your son passed away."

A son is a huge tree that is born in our chests. No matter the age of the child, the tree is already born big and strong.

10 August 1995

I woke up with just worries. I did not know how to reverse them in positive vibrations, I did not know that blessings are like a thin rain in people's hearts. Any other way, there was in me the essence of a Mom who, in recent months, overcame her fears and made me accept the life that pulsed within me. It is not that I did not feel love, but because the world is, very often, too cruel. Not even all the strength it has given to the lone female wolves is able to ensure the survival of the cubs.

I cried, cried a lot, a tight, silent cry, when I carried him in my arms for the first time. It was a painful happiness. I kissed him and loved him with all the intensity that a love can have.

Davi, a simple name, of course, that contains life in it, so I chose it. He fully fulfilled what it meant — what it means to me. The ex-husband came to meet his son, and, out of breath of that fragile moment when we want to believe in a fair possibility of living, this child brought us together again for another five years of hopes and stumbles.

Intelligent, curious, audacious, fearless, caring, creative, sensitive, fun, Davi grew up disconcerting the world around him to try to understand it.

During the sermon at a Sunday service in the neighborhood church, he, at the age of five, wanted to disagree with the priest. Asking a question for the fellowship to reflect about it, Davi understood that people were silent because they did not know the answer. He did, have an answer, and it was not an acceptance one, he had arguments. He was soon answering loudly: "I know!", causing surprised glances, which sought the owner of the sassy child's voice. I scolded him softly: "It's not meant to be answered, Davi, it's for you to think!", and he retorted, restlessly, softly, "I've thought about it and I have the answer." He did not accept the crucifixion of Jesus Christ. He thought that, as a son of God, He should have used his superpowers to get rid of his assassins.

We had already moved away from the bakery when I realized that he carefully held the candy, without having devoured it to satisfy his urgent desire as a child:

— Are you not going to eat the candy that the lady gave you?

— If I do, Israel won't have some.

— Oh, son, Israel is at school, you can eat it, he will get one later too — I tried to drive him away from guilt of not sharing with his brother such an important pleasure, in such a small candy.

— But the lady will leave, Israel won't get any candy.

— I am going to break it in half, okay? One half is for you, the other one you keep for Israel.

🎼

— Mom, I was thinking... We have no money, you made such a beautiful feather earring! Why don't you make a lot of feather earrings for me to sell at people's homes?

— Oh, my son... You are only seven...

— But I can sell it, I know how to sell!

🎼

— Mom, my essay has been chosen! I am going to participate in the exhibition at the Town Library! It is going to be in a magazine, the teacher said it!

🎼

— Mom, what is happiness to you? What is the point of life? Why are there so many bad things in this world?

🎼

To my father's family, I am rich; to my mom's family, I am poor. To my Dad's family I'm white; to my mom's family, I am black. I don't know who I am — he said laughing at his conclusion.

🎼

John, you like music, don't you? Why don't you quit this job and go work with music? Why don't you chase after your dreams, hard, willingly?

What about you, Mom? Why didn't you ever sing again, never played the guitar again?

— Wow! What a block I made today, Mom! It was like this, here, look at me: there was a guy from their team here, getting in the way, trying to block my vision, and the other kicked there from the right side, a strong kick! Then I just did like this, look! — he said repeating the gestures slowly, as if there was enough space in the room for that jump and the imaginary block on the ball in the corner of the goal, before throwing himself into bed, almost breaking it.

Davi needed space to be himself. When he was told he was not tall enough to be a professional goalkeeper, wanted to do treatment to grow taller. He did not take "no" for an answer, he went beyond the limits that kept him from finding out his very best. He would stretch as long as it took, not to let the ball in, not to lose the game of life; would give his all to celebrate with his team his victories and be as big as them.

A son is a replica of the universe that lives within us and then goes away without ever leaving.

Soap bubbles play in the backyard, transparent and deadly.

Hug me, hug me, hug me...

I paused for a second to repeat those words and make sure I understood them correctly, it could be a translation problem, while a cold ran through my body, making me weak.

— What? — I asked waiting for an answer to undo my deception.

— His body was found this morning.

— Did he kill himself?

— Yes, everything points that way.

— No, it can't be true!

Several thoughts arose, his message, the possibility of all that being a dream...I walked around the room, slapped my face repeating "this is a dream, this is a dream, it's not true. Wake up, Flávia, wake up!"

I went to the bathroom, locked the door, threw things on the floor in anger, broke the mirror repeating "this is a dream, this is a dream", out of myself, crying, screaming, "It's not true! That's not true! Davi! Davi...."

The cops were knocking on the door, another one came through the window, I was yelling at them to leave. I fell; without strength, a huge emptiness got hold of me, I had no ground or sky, I screamed without a voice: "Davi! Davi! Davi!...

A police officer broke down the door and several of them entered the bathroom. Me laying on the floor, in a corner near the bathtub, screaming with all my anger:

— Get out of here! Go work! Go save lives! You don't know how to work! You don't know! Useless! Get out of here! I asked you, I asked you many times to help my son! Incompetents! "Help, please, he's not well! He is suffering from a mental disorder! Help me, please! I'm alone!", and what did you do? Nothing! Nothing! Nothing! And now you come in here to tell me that my son is dead? Incompetents! Leave me alone! Get out of here! You and this fucking social assistance thing did absolutely nothing to help my son! The several times I asked, that I explained, that I begged... Everybody get out of here. Everybody get out of here, now!

I stayed there, laying down for hours, on the floor in tears so devastating that it was bursting everything inside, opening a huge hole, bottomless... I opened my eyes, someone was trying to talk to me, it was a paramedic, wanted to apply a sedative on me.

— Don't touch me! Get out of here!

I felt a big, strong tree being plucked from my chest, revolving the flesh with its roots, shaking everything, inside and out, creating a void that hurt unbearably.

Cops came in and out of the bathroom.

— Get away! There is nothing here for you to save!

Leticia sat next to me and stayed there until I completely cried everything out. Hours later, in my room, I found out that he had thrown himself off a cliff. I screamed, screamed, screamed... I wanted to go through time and space with my scream and stop him.

"No, Davi... No... No... No..."

I suffered my despair and his, together a desire to go along him, to be united, to suffer united, to die unitedly...

"I'm not going to leave you alone, son, I won't let you..."

Hours had passed...

How? Where is he? In peace, in the arms of the Lord? Suffering the consequences of taking his own life? How can a spirit still be punished after suffering so much? No, it didn't make sense to me. The only thing I could do at that moment was hold him hard in my thoughts.

Sitting on the bed, I leaned my head on the pillow against the wall. John came in, sat on the edge.

— Try to sleep.

— I don't want to sleep ever again so I don't have to wake up... I never want to wake up and relive it all over again. Don't let me sleep, please don't let me sleep...

I sobbed on my pillow and thought I might be having a nightmare and maybe it was better to sleep to wake up and see that all of that was a lie, to see Davi in his room, healthy, singing, happy.

𝄢

I was told that Joyce was coming from Brazil. I had to urgently find ways not to lose myself in that pain, even though I wanted to, even though thinking like that, diluted, I would find him. On the other hand, people "out there" needed to feel guided in my arms. Joyce, Israel, my parents and himself, Davi...

𝄢

I don't like the word "death." It is a dark word, full of pain and suffering. Passage is a word that doesn't hurt me. Passage is a bridge, a path that crosses to get to the other side.

For a few moments, I closed my eyes and felt the flight of a bird gliding in the immensity, light, confident. I needed to be him, I needed to be a bird.

Hole in the chest is no metaphor, and in it I fall into myself. No, I couldn't find any way out. Some friends came to help, brought warm words to guide me.

"Everything in this life is impermanent. We suffer when we cling to what is impermanent." I remembered this thought I had read a few times but had not absorbed as the necessity required. It made me feel better. I let it stay there, floating around. I closed my eyes repeating it, repeating it, repeating it, slowly, so that it wouldn't go away, so that it would stay there forever.

I did not want a deep sleep. The lamp lit and the position on the pillow, almost seated, gave me short and light naps.

Joyce arrived the next day, alone, a long and sad journey for such a lovely sister. We hugged and cried together at the door of the big house.

The coroner, the police officer in charge of Davi's case, had left a card asking me to contact him when I was able to. I called two days later, and we went, both of us, to his office at the police station. He, a friendly man, calmly told us that Davi's body was found, around six o'clock in the morning, on the seaside bike path, below the cliff between Brighton and

Ovingdean, by a man passing by on a bicycle. He said an inquiry would be opened to investigate that case of unnatural death. Asked me to write some information about Davi and email it to him. He handed us Davi's cell phone, wallet and a poem that were found a few feet from the scene.

I held the paper and started reading the poem. I felt myself entering it, in another dimension, every word guiding me into nothingness, feeling what I believed to be the same as Davi felt when writing it, experiencing his last steps, his breath.

> *"To see the world in a grain of sand*
> *and the sky in a wildflower,*
> *hold the infinity in the palm of your hand*
> *and eternity in an hour."*

The coroner's voice took me from that torpor: "These are the first verses of a famous poem by Englishman William Blake."

Joyce wanted to see the body, I did not. I did not want to see my son injured, but the coroner said the fractures were internal. Externally, he had only one bruise on his forehead. So, I fed on my daughter's strength and we went hand in hand together.

We crossed a garden and entered, just the two of us, in a small room through which light penetrated only through colorful stained-glass windows. In the center was his body, covered by a red robe and a white flower on his chest. I slid my fingers on his cold face and kissed him. An empty body..."Only" a body...

— His joyful spirit is free; he is at peace. Our prayers are guiding you, son, on a path of light and love.

The other day, we went to marina. We walked by the sea by the bike path within the cloudy afternoon. Between stones and a little sand, we left flowers, a candle and a prayer to brighten, illuminate and strengthen his path.

> *"May you always remember that God is your strength.*
> *He will always be holding your hand.*
> *Then teach your heart to fly because there is nothing to fear.*

The Lord is holding you, firmly.
You will forever be loved!" (unknown author)

Through these words, I saw the image of a hand welcoming him at the moment of the fall and his free spirit, in safe flight.

"It was just a manikin that fell." I kept with affection the explanation I heard from a child.

𝄢

The costs for a funeral were high. I had already spent all my credit card limit. I had almost nothing left. With the money his friends donated, we paid for the cremation. It was better that way; I wouldn't make that moment a spectacle of pain.

On the twenty-ninth of May, at eight-thirty in the morning, Joyce and I sat in the garden in front of the chapel at the Brighton crematorium. The morning was beautiful, a soft sun and a scent of wet grass calmed our hearts. Holding hands, we prayed and stood there for a long time watching the smoke rise, mixing with the clouds in the sky.

Later, we went down the cemetery road, surrounded by trees, until the avenue, where we took a bus to the city center. I needed to call the Consulate to expedite the documentation, but the street noise got in the way, so we went into the mall, where it was calmer. Outside a bookstore, a young man and a young woman came towards us, probably to sell something. I made a sign with my hand that was not interested and entered to make the call in a quiet corner. As soon as I finished, I saw a poster between the shelves: "Do you ignore people in crisis?". "No!" — I answered in a loud impulse and approached them to see what it was about. The boy, who I thought was a salesman, greeted me, and I was able to recognize the Red Cross slogan on his shirt. He began to explain the work of that organization as I looked at him more and more attentive. Kind of hypnotized, I noticed in his face similarities with Davi: the brown skin, the eyes, the eyebrow, the hair, the height, the way he moved. I was not even paying attention to what he was saying. Joyce also noticed the similarities and we looked at each other confirming our thoughts. I interrupted him by asking:

— How old are you?

He replied in a funny way:

— How old do you think I am?

— Nineteen.

— I am twenty.

— Where are you from?

He again reminded me of Davi, answering with questions:

— Where do you think I am from?

— I don't know... — I did not want to be so evident and say Brazil.

— A lot of people think I am Brazilian, but I am half African, half English.

— Oh, you do look Brazilian. We are Brazilians.

I filled out the form to make monthly donations to the Red Cross, with my eyes full of tears and a tighten heart... I wanted to hug him so badly and tell him how much he looks like my son who just passed away... I gave up the idea, I did not want to put him in an awkward situation, because I know I wouldn't be able to contain an immense cry trapped inside me. When I finished, he turned smiling and asked:

— Can I give you a hug?

— Ah... Please!!!

He hugged us, Joyce and I, like a disguised angel who was there just for that.

Preston Rock Garden is a small park with a stream, a lake, stones and gardens, on a small hill, in a region not far from the city center, full of peace and beauty, a small paradise. The day after the cremation, we took Davi's ashes there. We covered the grass with lacy white blankets, put flowers, candles and the pictures I had from when he was a kid. We spread thoughts and prayers, and hand in hand with the few friends who were able to attend, we prayed and thanked him for the opportunity to have him in our lives.

Chapter 14

Joyce returned to Brazil. She needed to return to her path, her work, her fiancé. What she planted in me was something that I had lost in between my storms, something she kept and made her grow stronger. I would be traveling in a few days. I was just waiting for the documentation to take Davi's ashes with me. I wanted to do this for him, for the love he had for Brazil, for his family, for his father, for the dear friends who were part of his life, who lived in him. I carried them with me, on my heart's lap, all night during the journey.

Israel is not a man of many words. Perhaps he learned to keep them as child, at that stage when many adults believe that kids can overcome everything. In there, within him, he built with them and with silences his ways and defenses. So, by having witnessed many falls, he learned to step on the places that seem safer to him.

I approached slowly:

— How are you, son?

— Fine.

— Wow... How hard it is to lose someone we love, isn't it? Stand strong, Israel! You know he wasn't well at all. He is now free from all that suffering...

— I know...

— Unfortunately, I was not able to get him any help... He was just getting worse and worse... Now we must accept his passage into the spirit world. We cannot get stuck in the past, we must move on with our lives in the best way, positively, it does him a lot of good. I want to ask you to set up a meeting with your father at Joyce's apartment. I want to tell him and you everything that happened.

I took some of Davi's belongings so that each one of them could choose what they wanted to keep as a reminder of Davi. They listened in silence; his father dissatisfied with the loss of his son:

— If he had stayed here...If he had not gone back to England...

— I have so many "ifs" inside me, so much guilt... Once the story ends, it is easy to come up with another ending, but while you are experiencing the drama, it is hard to see ways out. I was living a nightmare every day, submerged in tension. Every step was dubious, any of them could be fatal, and I was very afraid. I keep thinking that without any help as he was, the problems aggravating, the consequences could be even worse. With so many no's he had received during the years he lived in England, he could, in his sick mind, direct his frustrations to revenge on innocent people, as we have so often seen happen on television. But he solved it differently, "the Davi's way of being," and these people will never know that they had their lives at risk, at a school door, at a bus stop, in a park, on a sidewalk — just me. In this way too, no social assistant, no police officer, no doctor had their sleep night disturbed, his position shaken by a greater tragedy in the city. No one, no one.

From the emails between Davi and his father, I found out the seventh lawsuit against him, the process that I thought did not exist, that it was simply wrong math. It was Mike.

"Today I received another letter, now there are seven lawsuits! Seven! It was the Englishman who lives in the big house... But this one I don't even care about, because the cop saw it was not my fault. I just bumped my suitcase, unintentionally, on the television he left right in the middle of the way. Now he is saying it in here that I broke it..."

— Coward! — I said as I read that. — Taking revenge of me on my son. I remembered the scene: I was so confused, I preferred not to leave my room. I saw Davi come into the house with a policeman to pick up his things. I had washed all his clothes and packed his suitcase, lovingly, ruined with sadness. Mike had finally decided to move, was taking out his belongings and putting them in the car when Davi entered with the officer, took his suitcase, his backpack and left.

𝄢

After a ceremony that we named "Celebration of Davida" *(Davida-The combination of Davi + Vida, life in Portuguese)* with some family and friends, a young woman approached and said, "You don't know me, but I was very good friends with Davi." "If you were a very good friend of Davi, I should have met you." Later I looked her up on Facebook. I met with Laís Pires in the room where she gave ballet classes for children.

— I met Davi when I was seven or eight years old. We were from the same class. Our friendship began there. But at that time, I was going through some serious issues I had eating disorders and learning difficulties. It was motive for bullying for being chubby and having curly hair. I had some girl friends, but the boys, only came near to make fun of me, laugh and curse at me with offensive nicknames. In the midst of so many evil children, I met Davi, who was totally different, had a huge heart. I remember him clowning around and the whole class laughing, he loved to do that... He seemed like my older brother, calling me out, telling me to do the exercises, putting myself in his project group against the will of the other classmates. He never cared about my weight or my hair. He could see me beyond that. It was a very strong friendship. He was my biggest supporter, in everything, but especially in the things I love most, ballet and psychology. Whenever I was discouraged, he was there, giving me the strength to never give up. I rented this room a few months ago and I'm very happy to be able to make that dream come true. Soon, we will begin the *Project Davi*, offering dance classes to students who cannot afford it. There are several benefits in dancing, especially during the childhood. Through dance, it is possible to prevent and treat depression and various other psychic and biological problems. If you give these children a meaning, a love, a passion.... If you give them the chance to be good, to conquer, to reach something, you will already be preventing any psychic diseases that, later in life, can develop to a destructive form.

"What a beautiful person," I thought to myself. So young, going through a period of great responsibility, setting up her studio with financial difficulties, turbulence in personal life and yet donating her time, her knowledge and her love to heal such an important piece of the world.

At the Vine Mountain (Serra do Cipó), was where we his father, Joyce, Israel, and me decided to throw Davi's ashes. His friends Bel, Laís and Victor followed us in the farewell and liberation ritual. Bia was there too as a sunflower without sun. She was always there for him. They have never totally lost contact. There was a special light around them, holding them together. "Take care of yourself... Don't get lost" — was Davi last message to her.

At the entrance to the forest reserve, I donated a white flower plant. A young man made the record and said, "You can come back and see where it was planted. You can visit it whenever you want." We thought that the idea of visiting a plant was beautiful.

— Write in there that the name of this plant is Davi — his father requested.

We walked along a trail, near a river, until we found a small sandy bank. We went down helping each other carry our strong memories. I asked to read a few parts from a recently psychographed letter.

"My Mom Flávia,

(...) I need to feel embraced by your forgiveness, for the sadness I have caused you, and the feeling of helplessness and depression that has covered you with unfortunate comments that you have often heard about me.

(...) Thank you, Mom, for defending me at all times, even though I did not deserve it.

(...) I know your heart has forgiven me.

(...) That this feeling of guilt that is not true, but that you bring within you in your heart, dissipates.

(...) I affirm you that the suicidal is not eternally condemned to suffer by God. The suicidal (...) is a priority in the merciful eyes of God.

160

(...) No, Mom, your son isn't 'poeting' here.

(...) Accept the son who puts himself in this life in the condition of an apprentice.

(...) Thank you, Mom, for not killing me in your heart, that is what matters to me.

Keep moving forward, Mom, everything is going to be okay.

I wish to send memories and peaceful vibrations to my siblings.

Kisses from your son, that is always yours,

Davi"

We passed the urn from hand to hand. Each one took out a handful of ashes and threw it into the water. The wind made drawings with it in the air. We heard the snaps when it would fell on the water surface.

Inside us, an immensity: the fragility of life.

The silence and peace of nature condensed at that moment, like eternity in an hour. Every tree, every leaf, every breath, every cloud, every stone, every grain of sand, every wildflower, every drop of water has welcomed you completely, in a ceremony of perfect communion with the Universe.

I held infinity on the palm of my hand.

'And the river follows its course, until one day it ceases to be a river to become sea.'

Chapter 15

I went back to England. Wanted to be present at the inquiry's conclusion and calmly define what direction I would give to my life. I went back to the big house in Brighton, with Fred sleeping next to my sadness, Davi's pictures, his belongings... On my cell phone, his last message: "I'm not a sucker."

He knew that in the hearing the problems he was trying so much to hide would be exposed. He felt trapped. Under medical care, he would have his privacy respected and his illness treated privately. Two, if only two symptoms had been considered, things could have ended quite differently: suicidal thinking and obsession on not revealing his illness.

I remembered one of the first shows I watched on English TV. I did not contain the admiration and I told many times later in my conversations: "How much respect for life there is in here! How much respect!" At the scene, a dove, under an overpass, trapped on a grille, struggled to free itself without being able to do it. The animal protection agency was called in, and they soon sent a car with two agents who cut the wire, examined the bird, took care of its injuries and then released it.

There were messages from the Pastor on my cell phone that I did not read. A friend came to tell me he wanted to pay me a visit.

— Please don't let him come here. I cannot handle this situation yet. I don't want to be rude. To me, he's not religious. Maybe one day he will be able to be. I need to pray for him.

𝄢

On the morning of the inquiry's conclusion, I passed through the gates and went up the street that gives access to the crematorium. I entered the stone house, in silence. I did not see anyone else there. In the courtroom, just me, the coroner and the judge. I relived sad moments under the police point of view. One of the goals of that session was to rule out all the chances of a murder, to find out if Davi was involved with anyone or anything illicit that might have led him to that situation, such as crimes or gangs. Invisible monsters and omission of help were not on the agenda, because there was help, yes, first class, first world. A helicopter was sent to try to resuscitate him. I thanked in prayer the police and paramedics who came forward that morning of May 23, 2015 below the cliff.

Later, talking to a police officer, describing Davi's symptoms, she interrupted me:

— Did he use Cannabis?

— Yes, he was not an addict, but he did.

She shook her head, confirming her hypothesis.

— Yes... — I thought to myself — it wouldn't have been hard for them to put together the few pieces of this puzzle if they had listened to me, if they had investigated.

Chapter 16

John tried to continue our relationship, bought tickets to some places I always desired to visit, wanting to cheer me up. I was getting more and more distant. I knew my time there was running out. England did not make sense to me anymore. After weeks of not meeting up, I received a message:

— How long are you going to be like this?

— Forever. One day I am going to leave, John. So, feel free to restart your life.

This time he did not insist, he let me go.

A friend invited me to the National Spiritualist Church in Brighton. I went back there several times to pray and receive blessings. I gradually got to know the nice and welcoming people. There were individual psychic sessions every month, and even though I knew the meeting I was hoping for could not happen, I was there. It was early January, more than seven months since Davi had passed. I sat facing the medium, a cheerful, friendly lady, who I only knew by sight. Like all the people there, I had never talked to any of them, just greeted them.

She began by saying that there were, in spirit, a man of my family core and also a lady, who, by the descriptions, I identified as my maternal grandma and grandfather.

— They have come to bring you love — said the medium –, she is doing the sign the cross, which means she is very catholic. She is trying to say something about a car. Do you have a car?

— I had one.

— Did something happen to this car? Any accidents?

— No...

— Maybe later this will make sense. There is also a boy here, good looking, dark skin, brown eyes, a close family member — she continued.

— It is my son Davi – I replied very moved.

— He is very witty, playful, but he has also another side, quiet, introspective, depressive... He said that people did not see this side of him and that it was very difficult for them to understand what happened... He said he did not want to kill himself; it was the disease. He is saying that he loves football, that you put a small portrait of him, in a picture frame; placed flowers and candles in a place where you always pass by and always talk to him, pray to him... He says he receives your prayers and thanks you, that he is sorry for everything he has done. The car... There was a problem with the car!

— Oh, yes... His car... He crashed it into a traffic sign. The police seized it and destroyed it.

— He said it could have been much worse, that he could have been involved in a serious accident... Said that at the celebration, there were friends of him that you did not know. Says he is by your side and wants you to send his love to his brothers, sister and father. Your grandma is saying she is looking out for him.

Weeping, I thanked my loved ones for coming to meet me and the beautiful lady, the medium.

— I will always keep praying, son.

I went into the bathroom to wash my face and cried, cried, cried... I thought about why my grandma seemed so distressed when she tried to say something about the car. Maybe she intervened, avoiding a tragedy.

On the morning of my departure, I realized I left the computer on. I slept listening to music. When I opened it up, there was a Pink Floyd video ready to play. Eclectic, Davi liked the band. I read the name of the song while trying to unravel coincidences: *Learning to Fly*. I did not know it. I pressed play.

Oh, Davi, I cried all over again... You and your strong flights... The lone man, mowing a huge field of wheat, being consumed by it. The flight, the voice, the feather, the jump... I yelled softly at him not to jump, but he needed to learn how to fly.

> *"No navigator to find my way home*
> *Unladened, empty and turned to stone*
> *A soul in tension that's learning to fly*
> *Condition grounded but determined to try*
> *Can't keep my eyes from the circling skies*
> *Tongue-tied and twisted just an earth-bound misfit, I"*

𝄢

I hugged Fred feeling a river bursting inside me... I held back fast; I wouldn't be able to endure it.

— Thank you, John, for staying with Fred. Thank your girlfriend for me. Life will reward you.

𝄢

I arrived in Brazil alone, with empty pockets and a broken heart. "Be firm" — I said to myself. "This is where I'm going to plant my longing."

After ten years away, fragile as I was, it was not easy, I could not readapt. A year later, battling depression, I borrowed some money and left to save myself.

𝄢

Snowdonia is a national park in north Wales, scenery of some paradise, formed by mountains and lakes. The simple work at the old inn and a trailer to share with a Romanian woman, a few meters away, were enough for me to start over.

There were sick questions, missed steps and masts with no flags inside me. I took the laptop and started writing my story, our story, Davi's story. I spent the winter locked in my little room, a little bigger than the bed. Gradually, the writing was getting painful and my fingers could no longer press the keys. His voice repeated in my memory: "Don't tell anyone about anything, no one!" I waited a few days in silence for some sign, some intuition, which we call the "voice of the heart". I wanted to go to the National Spiritualist Church. I found one in Coventry, three hours away by train. Mark Brandist was the medium who welcomed me that night, with a tender, welcoming smile. I felt his clear aura. I sat in an armchair in front of him in a small room. He asked me:

— Would you like to connect with someone specifically?

— Yes, I would.

He closed his eyes, took a deep breath and waited a few moments.

— There is in here in the room a lady, a gentleman and a young man. How long has the person you want to communicate with passed away?

— Two and a half years.

— The boy is making this sign — he drew it in the air, with his finger, the letter D.

I smiled. I felt tears wetting my face.

— He is sending you kisses.

— I love you, son!

— He has very beautiful eyes. He is showing his head. He had a problem with his head.

— Yes, he did.

— He is saying that he is clean now, that life on Earth was very difficult for him, that his problem was very fast, that now he is free of everything, healed! He is very witty, playful. He said that he likes to play football in heaven! — said the medium, finding it amusing.

— What a joy to know...

We continued connected for about 15 minutes. Before finishing up the meeting, the medium closed his eyes for a few moments and asked me:

168

— Would you like to ask any questions?

I felt immensely relieved to hear that. I spent the whole trip thinking about how to approach the subject, if I could, during the meeting, ask a question; if I had the meeting, if I had the answer, a message, a sign at least that made me believe that I could write the book the way I was doing it, exposing his lines, his life, his illness. So, there was the opportunity, the door all open, putting an end to my worries. Spiritual connections...

— Yes. I want to ask if I can tell everything that happened to him in the book I am writing. I want his permission.

— Everything! — answered bluntly. — You can tell everything! He said that this book is going to help a lot of people.

A feeling of peace and happiness got hold of me completely. How nice to feel him like this, joyful, complete, healed!

Mark Brandist gave me a loving hug. I said, crying on his shoulder.

— He is my beloved son!

— I know... I want to read your book when it is ready.

— And I want to read yours! — he told me that he was also writing one. I walked down the street feeling a drumming noise tuning my heart. A melody was being born in there.

I hummed softly, muffling the no's:

Hold this flag

Raise this flag

Spread this flag

𝄢

Duringlonely attempts to understand what was happening to Davi, I searched the internet and found important texts, studies, descriptions of mental illnesses that I sought to associate with my observations about his speech, his behavior, his distorted perception of reality at various dark moments that unintentionally appeared in his mind. Eighteen months since an important depression that was presenting other characteristics. In the face of several coincidental aspects, I would say that he may have suffered from schizoaffective disorder. Thought disorder, perception disorder, disturbances in emotions, loss of the ability to feel pleasure (typical states of severe depression), demotivation, social isolation, delusions (persecution, paranoia, feeling of being greater or false superior, nihilism), low self-esteem, suicidal thoughts and substance use are some symptoms of schizoaffective disorder,**[1] is made "crucial" in which an evaluation of the risk that the patient offers to himself and others. Given the possible difficulty in obtaining information from the patient himself, it is necessary to interview family members and known people** (my emphasis).

The Schizoaffective disorder is a chronic disease that affects 0.3% of the world population. Most cases manifest between late adolescence and early adulthood. The causes may be related to problems during pregnancy and childbirth, as well as genetic, neurobiological factors, psychological, social processes, stress and substance use. Schizoaffective disorder can be treated efficiently with medication and psychotherapy. Patient adherence and family participation are fundamental for the recovery, in part or completely, of their social, productive and functional capacities.

*D*avi, I wanted so much that you and so many people could have had a chance to understand, that... There are ways out! If your mind is telling you there is not, don't believe it. If your mind has painted the world dark gray and is telling you that it is an unbearable place, that you are nothing, you are nobody, don't believe it. It is trying to trick you. Fight the invisible monsters that are acting to change your perception of reality. Fight tirelessly with all existing medications and treatments until you find the most appropriate ones. Throw to the ground this barrier that is keeping you from acting and tell the people you trust, "I need your help." Tell them everything. Seek professionals. Summon your army. Break stigmas. Destroy monsters. Arrest them. Master them. You are bigger than them!

I wanted you to understand that I will always be there for you.
The world needs wonderful people like you.
I need you.

Pathways require my steps
cover themselves up of answers to live

Sewing up flags on my path
infinite colors
infinite love

Tattooing onto myself, respect, yearning
his smiles, his stares

Drums, clear the way!
make my soul vibrate
make the wind blow
make the flag fly and spread

Play, drums
of all the suffering
free myself of my unreal thoughts
and trap them where they can't reach me
for my eyes encounter light
for my steps encounter ground

Play, drums
dissolve this loneliness
penetrate my heart
evaporate all the unbearable pain

Play over my true self
where I am me, wholly
Play about my strength
and about my happiness

Play, drums
about motorways, about railways

at the pubs, at the clubs
at the hospitals, at the police stations
at the churches, temples and cathedrals

Play, drums
through every road and avenue
in the villages, cities and outskirts
over the statues, monuments
over schools and prisons
over the parliament
over the royal palaces

Play, drums
on the billboards, over your voicemail
on your TV, on your pillow

Over the rocks at the beach
over the water of the sea

Fly, drums, around the world
voice of drums through the air

Drums and flags

Acknowledgments

I thank everyone who has helped me, somehow,
to build this book: to my parents, children, relatives and friends.
To Sonia Palma, Raphael Menezes, Marcus Vinícius Menegaz,
Duncan Beamont, and, specially Dilce Laranjeira.

I also want to thank to all of those who will make of this
book an act of change.

References about Schizoaffective Disorder

1. BOTA, Robert G., PREDA Adrian, Schizoaffective Disorder, *BMJ Best Practice*, 2019. Available at: <https://bestpractice.bmj.com/topics/ptbr/1199?q=Transtorno%20esquizoafetivo&c=suggested>. Accessed 28 February 2019.

2. BRASIL. Ministério da Saúde. Secretaria de Atenção à Saúde. Portaria No 1203, 04 nov. de 2014. Protocolo Clínico e Diretrizes Terapêuticas. Transtorno Esquizoafetivo. Portal Arquivos 2. Available at: <http://portalarquivos2.saude.gov.br/images/pdf/2014/novembro/06/Publica----o-nov2014-Transtorno-Esquizoafetivo.pdf>. Accessed 30 January 2019.

3. D'SOUZA, Deepak et al. Efeitos comportamentais, cognitivos e psicofisiológicos dos canabinóides: relevância para a psicose e esquizofrenia, *Scielo*. Available at: <http://www.scielo.br/scielo.php?script=sci_arttext&pid=S1516-44462010000500005>. Accessed 2 March 2019.

4. ERICKSON, Rafaella. Quais os sintomas do transtorno esquizoafetivo? *Médico Responde*. Available at: <https://medicoresponde.com.br/quais-ossintomas-do-transtorno-esquizoafetivo>. Accessed 30 January 2019.

5. SCHIZOAFFETIVE disorder. *Mental Health*. Available at: <http://mentalhealth-uk.org/help-and-information/conditions/schizoaffective-disorder/>. Accessed 23 October 2019.

6. SCHIZOAFFETIVE disorder. *Mind*, May 2019. Available at: <https://www.mind.org.uk/information-support/types-of-mental-health-problems/schizoaffective-disorder/#.XbBsivZFyP8>. Accessed 23 October 2019.

7. SCHIZOAFFETIVE Disorder. *Nami*. Available at: <https://www.nami.org/learn-more/mentalhealthconditions/schizoaffective-disorder>. Accessed 2 March 2019.

8. TRANSTORNO esquizoafetivo: história, sintomas e tratamento. *A mente é maravilhosa*, 19 de maio de 2018. Available at: <https://amenteemaravilhosa.com.br/transtorno-esquizoafetivo/>. Accessed 2 January 2019.

About the Author

Flávia Menegaz, born in Belo Horizonte, Brazil, in 1964. Graduated in Languages, with Graduate studies in Portuguese Language, she was a teacher and coordinator of a reading room in a Brazilian publishing house. In 2005, her book *Poetando* (Alis, 2003), was selected by PNBE – National School Library Program. In 2006, moved to England where, among other activities, worked voluntarily disseminating the cultures of Brazilian indigenous societies.

Recently Flávia resumed her poetic side, releasing *Reversos*, with illustrations by Dilce Laranjeira. Autonomous, she is dedicated to the publication of her books in several countries, and especially to suicide prevention.

Printed in Great Britain
by Amazon